The A

R'gal
the Archangel

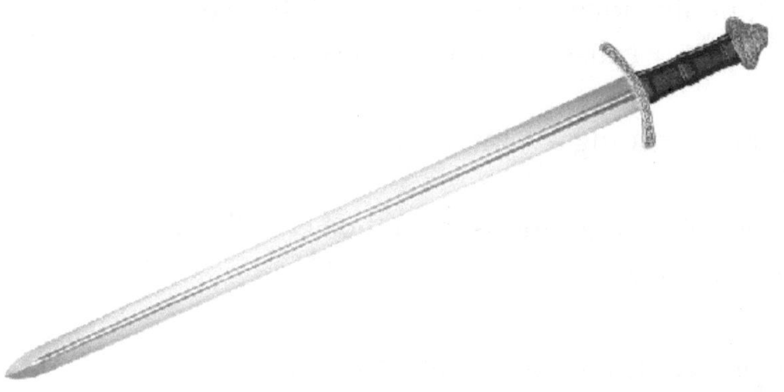

Book One -
The Sword of Shenah

By William Siems

ISBN: 979-8-9853654-8-1

First printing - Winter 2022

Scripture quotations from the SUV (Siems Unauthorized Version) of the Bible

Contact the author at chayeem10@gmail.com

Cover by Jacob Bridgman

Interior design by Alane Pearce of Professional Writing Services LLC contact at apearcewriting@gmail.com

Dedication

I thought I would write a novel. It took forty-five years. Its sequel came much faster, followed by a trilogy. Who would have thought? As I have developed the Siems Fantasy Universe I have discovered some holes. An effort to fill one of them has resulted in this current volume. Again, without the faithful support of so many people this would still be a hole. Thanks again to my wife, Nancy, who was my constant inspiration and encouragement. She hears each chapter in its rough draft form. My daughter, Angela, is my primary editor and attacks her task with what I would call "compassionate severity." She usually asks, "What color would you like to see a lot of this time?" Finally, there is the center of it all, Jesus. You may encounter Him as a Tree, the young man Rayeh, or…

For seven of the fifteen years I taught full-time at Boeing Airplane Company, Gil Henry was my partner. Those were incredible years. I have never had a teaching partner his equal. In the late 1990's he drew me a bookmark which was adapted for the cover of Hane and the Centurion. I have included here one of his other drawings to depict a young version of the Tree, Chayeem. He has taken the "ultimate upgrade" (Heaven), but I'm pretty sure he is pleased, both with this book and that his art is included (used with permission from his wife).

Preface

The trilogy of the Chayeem Chronicles is considered a Biblical Adventure: a portion of the Christmas story, a re-telling of the Life of Jesus (William's version of the Gospel), and a recounting of the first part of the Book of Acts (the life of Barnabas). The exact genre of this current volume is more difficult to establish. While parts of it are loosely based off of a Biblical narrative, most of it is just fantasy adventure or speculative fiction. Written from the perspective of an angel and beginning before the start of just about everything, you will have to grant me some poetic license, ie., "How does he know that what he is looking at is a tree? He has never seen one before."

Blessings…

William Siems, Fall 2022

Table of Contents

Prologue

His hands covered his eyes. The light was nearly blinding as he opened them a little at a time. It took a moment, even then, for them to adjust as he peeked beneath his cupped palms to gaze at his feet. He seemed to be standing on a floor of polished white marble. Even that was difficult to look at directly. His eyes adjusted some more until squinting he could remove his hands and then let them drop slowly to his sides. He felt unmistakable awe. His feet were bare, he wore no clothing, as he slowly filled his lungs again and again with the purest of air. He slowly let his eyes wander forward. There, about twenty cubits before him, stood a pillar of fire about twenty-five cubits in diameter. It began at the marble floor and reached to the firmament above him. The pillar radiated heat, but not unbearably so. He should have been enveloped in terror. A raging pillar of fire stood directly before him, yet his entire being, engulfed in awe, reacted by slowly driving him to his knees in reverence. There could be nothing like this in all that existed. This was the epitome of holiness.

Then he felt the voice, the first speech he had ever heard, sounding like what it must feel like to be home, to be in that place where you felt most wanted, where you felt you belonged. The voice said,"R'gal, you may enter the pillar of fire."

His mind reeled, *"What? This is a real pillar of fire, not just some illusion."* However, everything inside of him calmly replied, "This voice can be trusted above all others." Without another thought, he stood up and stepped into the pillar of fire to discover… a tree, twice the height of a man. R'gal looked at the base of the tree, wondering, *"How could a tree be rooted in a floor of marble?"* only to find that the ground inside of the pillar was not marble, but grass cropped short.

The tree rose up out of the grass. The holiness inside of the pillar intensified even more and R'gal was on his way to his knees again when he realized that something or someone sat in the branches of the tree. It was a young boy. R'gal stopped kneeling and stood back up.

The Tree spoke, "R'gal, let me introduce myself. I have many names, but you can address me as Ha….ha….ha..ha.. hahahaha."

"Laughter, your name is, laughter?" He found it difficult to address the Tree at all, but the laughter had made it easier.

If a Tree could smile, the atmosphere seemed filled with smiles, and the lad added to it by smiling broadly himself. The Tree continued, "Or, if we are being formal, Chayeem will do quite nicely, and this is Rayeh."

The boy slipped out of the tree to land gracefully on the grass. He took two steps forward, wrapped his arms around R'gal's waist, and laid his head on a stunned R'gal's chest, saying a muffled, "It's nice to meet you." After holding on for a moment, the boy stepped back and looked up to R'gal, straight into his eyes. "Huh, you have one blue eye and one green eye. How marvelous."

R'gal swallowed and inhaled deeply, "Nice to meet you … too."

Rayeh released R'gal, turned away from him, and held his right hand back towards him. "Let's go meet the others." R'gal took Rayeh's hand with his left and was pulled beneath Chayeem's branches. Rayeh gently slapped Chayeem's trunk with his left hand as they passed it with a, "We'll see you in a bit," and pulled R'gal outside of the pillar of fire.

On the other side of the pillar of fire, the grass that had been under the Tree extended across a meadow into a forest of luscious green-blue firs that stretched up into the surrounding hills. In the middle of the meadow stood a centaur, a massive, exquisite black stallion whose head was the upper torso of a well-muscled man in his prime. The centaur held some items in his hands that were difficult to distinguish at this distance.

Rayeh raised a hand calling out, "Alathos, we're here!" As Alathos casually walked towards them, Rayeh called, "This is R'gal, the last of them I believe."

"Welcome R'gal, we have been waiting for you," and he nodded almost in deference. There was something incredibly majestic, powerful, and mysterious about Alathos and his voice contained an authority that rivaled the Tree's.

R'gal nodded in return as he looked around. *"Who is we?"* he thought. There was no one else in view.

"Things are pretty simple here." Alathos held out a plain white robe to him and a matching white multi-corded rope to tie around his waist. R'gal donned the robe and secured it with the rope. Alathos' smile was as disarming as his voice. "I'll take you to the others. It will be easier to ride on me than to follow behind me," he added, "if you don't mind."

Rayeh stepped up next to Alathos' flank, interlocked his cupped fingers to provide a step for R'gal, and cocked his head toward Alathos' back. The implication was clear. With his left hand R'gal grasped a small patch of mane where Alathos' long hair ended and the body of the horse began, placed his right hand on Alathos' back, stepped into Rayeh's hands, and swung his leg over to straddle the centaur's back like he'd been doing it all of his life. He then reached down to grasp Rayeh's forearm and swung him up to ride behind him. Alathos seemed unfazed by the extra weight as he called over his shoulder, "Shall we?"

Rayeh reached back to slap Alathos on the flank, "Giddey up!" Alathos just shook his head, as Rayeh whispered over R'gal's shoulder, "I've always wanted to do that."

They began at a walk then advanced to a trot. R'gal had never ridden a horse before, let alone a centaur. He was surprised how easily it came to him.

All of these new experiences, one after another had him echoing Rayeh's, "How marvelous!"

The path through the trees was almost a road. It would have accommodated four or five horses riding abreast. He wondered if there were horses. Then he wondered how he even knew what a horse was.

He calmly asked Alathos, "Are there more centaurs? Is that who we are going to meet?"

"You asked two questions and there are multiple answers. Yes, there are more centaurs. No, we are not going to meet any more of them right now. I am taking you to meet more of you." He paused, contemplating a question of his own. He questioned in his heart if he should ask it and heard a definite, "Certainly" response in his own heart. "R'gal, do you know what you are?"

R'gal looked at himself, imagining he looked quite majestic in his white robe, riding a centaur, with a young boy behind him gripping him around the chest. Surely there must be a name for his kind, but nothing sprang to mind. He smiled, unconcerned, "Nope, do you?"

Alathos listened again for permission to proceed and received it. "You are an angel. More precisely, an archangel, a leader of other angels."

R'gal felt a strange warming of his heart. "An archangel, I'm an archangel."

PART ONE
It Begins

Chapter One
The Others

They turned a corner to find a break in the forest that opened to a sunlit meadow, also of closely cropped grass that reminded him of the grass that the Tree had grown out of in the pillar of fire. Suddenly it felt like they were entering an atmosphere of holiness again. He had not noticed any difference once they passed out of the pillar away from the Tree, but something must have been different at least in its intensity because it now felt like they were entering extreme holiness again.

Alathos had stopped. As R'gal looked up the meadow, he could just make out a number of other figures on a small rise. Alathos spoke and his words radiated warmth, "The others are waiting for you R'gal. Rayeh and I have been asked to return to the Tree."

He was more curious than afraid. "Who are… they?"

Rayeh shimmied back on Alathos' rump to give R'gal room to dismount. "More like you, but they look like men," Rayeh said simply.

R'gal bent his knee, swung it over Alathos' back and slid to the ground. He stepped forward to look up into Alathos' eyes. "Thank you." He felt he missed his new friend already.

Alathos smiled. "You will see us again," and he reached a hand down towards R'gal.

R'gal reached up and Alathos grasped his forearm. He grasped back, "See you soon, I hope."

He waved, "Bye," to Rayeh, turned on his heel and strode briskly up the hill towards the men.

Six of them reclined around a low table of food and drink. He suddenly felt hungry, thirsty too. That seemed odd, but maybe not. A lot had been going on since he had opened his eyes into this world. He had not had much time to think about eating and drinking. All six of them got to their feet, quite lithely, and almost as one. They could have been brothers, or at least closely related. They were all tall, of similar height and build, and each wore a white robe as he did.

The man nearest him laughed as he stepped forward. Perhaps he was their spokesman. "Another white-robed figure. We were hoping for a bit of a change. I'd say you were late, but then we didn't know when to expect you, only that you were coming." He reached out a hand. "I'm Gabriel." He lowered his voice, "Some say I talk too much," and he chuckled.

"R'gal," and he grasped Gabriel's forearm. He hoped that was appropriate. To say that Gabriel's grasp was firm would be an understatement.

"Ah, 'God's friend,' that is the interpretation of your name. Let me introduce my brothers," another chuckle. Gabriel continued, "This is Michael, he thinks he looks the most like our Father." Michael stepped forward, his arm extended, and they too grasped forearms. "And Uriel, he's quite light on his feet. Uriel means 'the light of God.'" Another forearm grasp. "This is Raphael, he keeps trying to tell us which of the fruit," and he pointed to the table, "is the healthiest. Then there is Raziel, he's a little mysterious, and Haniel, our resident comedian." R'gal grasped each of their forearms in turn also. "Come join us at the table." There were cushions on the grass, one for each of the seven of them, with one left over at the head of the table. "So, R'gal, what do you know?"

As R'gal sat, Haniel grabbed a golden pitcher from the center of the table, then R'gal's goblet, and asked, "Some juice?" as he winked.

"Yes, please." R'gal was suddenly very thirsty.

"Oh," Haniel smiled, "you don't have to be formal. We're all family. Although," and he looked at Raziel, "the courtesy is nice." Raziel just shook his head back and forth.

"Wow! That's pretty heady stuff!" R'gal had taken a large drink from the crystal goblet.

Haniel winked again. "We're all trying to pace ourselves. We're not sure if we can get drunk, but regardless, we feel that it wouldn't be… appropriate."

R'gal shook his head slowly, took a couple deep breaths, and looked across the table to Gabriel. "I don't know very much. I woke up, entered a pillar of fire to meet the Tree, Chayeem, and the boy, Rayeh. Rayeh took me out of the pillar to meet Alathos and we rode him through the forest to here. Oh, Alathos said I was an angel, an archangel."

"Oh," Gabriel looked at the others, "he's an archangel." He put a lot of emphasis on the word 'archangel.' Then he smiled again, "It's okay. We're all archangels. What do you think that means?"

"Alathos also mentioned something about leading other angels."

"So, there must be more than just the seven of us? Or eight," and he nodded towards the empty cushion.

"I guess. Have you," and he looked around the table, "met other angels? What are we exactly?" R'gal questioned.

Gabriel kept talking. "Angels are messengers of the Tree, created to carry out his orders and commands. If you thought of it as an army and a hierarchy, there are the troops, the regular angels arranged hierarchically, and at the top of the pyramid are the generals, we archangels.

Haniel passed R'gal a plate of fruit and whispered, "He does carry on a bit."

"I heard that, Haniel," but Gabriel was smiling.

Haniel pointed to a large dark purple colored fruit, "Raphael says that's not good for you, but I think he's mistaken."

R'gal held the fruit out to Raphael, "What's wrong with this?"

Raphael humphed. "There's nothing 'wrong' with it," he stated firmly, "I just think it's too sweet to be really healthy." They did treat each other like family, friendly banter and all.

R'gal took a bite, juices dripping down his chin, "Wow! That is amazing!" Haniel pulled a napkin from under R'gal's plate and handed it to him as R'gal continued with his mouth full, muffled, "How could this not be healthy?" R'gal wiped his chin.

"Just my opinion!" Raphael made a face at Haniel.

Uriel addressed Gabriel. "Does he," nodding towards R'gal, "know why we are here?" R'gal shrugged his shoulders at Uriel as he shook his head, "No."

"This will be a time of training. We were created as angels, archangels, but we must grow into all of what that means."

"How do we do that?" questioned R'gal.

Gabriel stood up, stepped back from the table, and the others followed suit. Suddenly, Gabriel stood before them having grown proportionately from a well-built man, a little over four cubits tall dressed in a white robe, to a huge man of twice that size, with a set of glorious wings and fully dressed in battle armor.

R'gal stood there with his mouth open as one by one they all did the same. His eyes widened to match his mouth as he exclaimed, "How did you do that?"

"Lesson One on becoming you." Gabriel was smiling again. "Think of wings deep in your spirit and proclaim the word there, in your spirit, for the entire spirit-realm to hear."

"Wings?" R'gal questioned.

"In your spirit!"

"How do I do that?" he exclaimed.

"Remember when you stood before Chayeem?" R'gal nodded. "And you were at a loss for words?" He nodded again. "Go there again in your mind and say deep in your heart," Gabriel pointed to his chest, "Wings!"

R'gal closed his eyes to concentrate, pictured standing before Chayeem, and breathed deeply inside of himself the word *"Wings!"* It had almost been a whispered wish. He had been standing there looking up at all of them, but when he opened his eyes he was looking at them all on the same level. He looked downward. He was dressed for battle. He looked over his right shoulder...wings.

Haniel piped up, "He had to close his eyes. I told you he'd have to close his eyes!" He too smiled at R'gal. "We all did, except maybe Gabriel. He was the first of us, so there were no witnesses."

Gabriel was still smiling, "And the secret stays with me."

R'gal smiled in return, then something caught his attention. He pointed over Gabriel's head. Above the trees of the forest, something was coming towards them in the sky. "What is that?"

Chapter Two
Their Chief

Gabriel did not even turn around, "That would be Lucifer, our prince."

Haniel leaned over and whispered, "He's special." R'gal wondered what he meant.

The flight of an angel can be almost mesmerizing and Lucifer knew how to take full advantage of the spectacle. He tucked his wings in close and drove himself into a rapidly-spiraling descent. The sound accompanying his dive matched its visual effect. The wind across his body created a near symphony of sounds that harmonized into an increasing crescendo. It seemed he was going to crash right into them and R'gal stepped instinctively backwards as Lucifer unfurled his wings into a huge flap, halted the dive, and landed just before them.

As a deafening silence replaced the symphony, he spread his arms, bowed, and smiled. The difference about him took a moment to register. Lucifer did not wear battle armor, but a breastplate that shone of burnished gold and consisted of an intricate network of pipes and socketed jewels. The pipes had produced the music as he flew and a measure of it still accompanied his every breath and every word. His breastplate glittered with all manner of precious gems and stones, sparkling even as he stood still. He folded his wings and became a man who was also different somehow, even in his human form. His robe was not white, but royal blue. As if almost on command, the rest of them resumed their own human forms, all except R'gal, who didn't know how to do that yet.

Gabriel started to explain, "In order to reverse the process…."

Lucifer abruptly interrupted him, "I've got this Gabriel." He sounded a little condescending. "To learn to transform into an angel and sprout wings you say the keyword 'wings' while envisioning that you are standing before Chayeem. Now, you might think that the keyword to reversing the process might be something like, 'un-wings' or 'become human,' but it's not. It is to simply say the boy's name, 'Rayeh.' Try it!" He spoke it like a command.

R'gal tried it and nothing happened. "Nothing," he said, his eyes downcast.

Lucifer smiled, but it did not seem entirely genuine. "You may need to close your eyes." He seemed a bit disappointed. R'gal looked down, locked eyes with Lucifer, and instantly regained his human form.

"Hmmm," responded Lucifer looking around him, "None of the rest of you were able to do that the first time without closing your eyes." He said it flatly, with no hint of admiration.

However, the esteem of the other six archangels for R'gal definitely rose a few notches. Contrarily, Lucifer thought, *"I will have to keep my eye on this one."*

Regaining control, Lucifer added, "I passed Alathos on my way here. It seems he brings a surprise for us all. My, but I do like surprises." Lucifer smiled again. It still seemed false.

R'gal wondered, "Why?"

Chapter Three
Their Swords

Alathos did not stop at the edge of the meadow this time, but walked right up to stand in front of them. For some reason Lucifer seemed diminished in the presence of Alathos and the boy Rayeh, who again sat astride his back. Alathos pulled behind him a tall wheeled cart, as tall as his back. He and the boy dragged it by two long poles, their hands together holding each of the poles. Rayeh released the poles and gracefully slid under the right one to drop silently from Alathos' back. He went behind the centaur, reached up high to brace the poles as Alathos released them, and stepped out of them. Alathos slowly turned to the left and walked back around towards the cart. Along the way he stopped and unfastened each of the poles, part way to the cart, and allowed them to fold down to the ground in such a way that they braced the cart in a nearly perfectly horizontal position. He moved to the side of the cart itself and reverently folded back the veil covering it. Rayeh moved to the opposite side of the cart to assist him. Light coalesced to sparkle off the objects in the cart, creating quite a spectacle.

There was a corporate gasp by the angels who had formed a semi-circle around Rayeh's side of the cart.

Alathos' voice took on a sing-song quality, "It will be said in the times to come that seven singing swords were forged for the archangels before time began." He paused. "These are those swords." He smiled, "There is an eighth, but it will not be part of that legend." He paused again then called out, "Lucifer, step forth."

Lucifer almost cringed at the sound of that command. He was not used to being told what to do by anyone. Yet he complied, and stepped out of the semi-circle towards Rayeh. Reverence covered Alathos like a garment as he reached his hands into the cart, retrieved a sword, and handed it across the cart to Rayeh's hands, extended palms up. Rayeh slowly pivoted to face Lucifer and almost sternly whispered, "Kneel." Again, that slight moment of reluctance, but he complied. Lucifer went to one knee and held out his hand palms up to receive the sheathed sword.

Rayeh spoke and his words twinkled even more beautifully than Lucifer's music. "The blessing of him who was, and is, and is to come, rest upon you and this sword. I give you 'Helel,' the bright star," and he laid the sword in Lucifer's waiting hands. Something powerfully fell upon Lucifer as the sword touched his palms, so powerful that he almost collapsed under the weight of it. He took a deep shuddering breath and struggled to his feet. The whispered command resounded again, "Draw the sword!" Lucifer quickly drew it from its sheath to reveal a blinding light that made all of the angels take a step backwards and cover their eyes. Its sound was beyond description, but Lucifer held it aloft and basked in its radiance, his jewels sparkling in all directions.

Alathos spoke from the other side of the cart, "I call you Halel, wielder of Helel. Step into your destiny as the conductor and choreographer of worship for the cosmos. You are the first, the foremost, but not the last. Behold, Chayeem has prepared a place for you." For a moment longer Halel stood there in the beauty of the sword held high. Then a momentary puzzled look crossed his face as he brought the sword down, sheathed it, and threaded it through the cord around his waist. He stepped back whispering to himself, "but not the last?" as a portal opened to his right. Halel pivoted to his right and stepped through it. "Join the stones of fire," Alathos' voice echoed down through the portal and it closed. There was a moment of silence, stillness, and all the angels inhaled slowly.

Alathos called out, "Gabriel," and that is all he said before Gabriel had enthusiastically stepped forward to take a knee in front of Rayeh. He bowed his head. Rayeh turned to Alathos and the cart to receive another sword. He then turned back to Gabriel, holding another shining sword and scabbard towards him.

"Gabriel," Rayeh commandingly whispered, "You are my strength. I give you Kol, the sword of thunder." Gabriel looked up, reached out his hands to receive the sword, but Rayeh was not through. "There is another characteristic of you and this sword that seems almost contradictory yet is not. It is 'tender.' Hmmm, tender thunder," and he placed the sword in Gabriel's hands.

The awe he felt was palpable, as wonder spread over his face, coalescing into the tears that filled his eyes. He barely got the words out, "Thank you." He bowed his head again and struggled up from his knee. He started to unsheathe the sword, thought better of it, and instead threaded the sword and scabbard through the cord at his waist and stepped back into the semi-circle. No portal opened.

Alathos called, "Michael." Michael smiled, looked left and right at his fellow archangels, and stepped forward. R'gal had not noticed it before, probably because he had never seen them this close together, but Michael looked like an older reflection of Rayeh. It was uncanny. Michael took a knee.

"Michael," began Rayeh, "I've heard Gabriel jokingly say to your brothers that you think you are the one who looks the most like our father. Is that true?" Michael dropped his head, but also nodded. Rayeh continued, "That's funny, I think I look most like him." Michael lifted his head showing his grin. "Regardless, we do have a singing sword for you." Rayeh turned to Alathos, who handed him another sword. He turned back to Michael and held it out to him. "'Eshair' a questioning of who, what. Questions are not the same as doubts. Doubts darken the truth; questions seek to bring the truth into the light. You may stand and unsheathe it."

Michael first looked deep into Rayeh's eyes and mouthed, "Thank you." Then he slowly stood, widened his stance, and in one fluid motion unsheathed Eshair. It was another indescribable moment, not one filled with questions, but as though the entire cosmos responded with a single, monumental, "YES!" He stood there as the atmosphere reverberated with echoes of certainty bouncing all around. He took a deep breath, re-sheathed the sword, and stepped backwards into the semi-circle.

Alathos called forth Raphael, who also stepped forward to take a knee before Rayeh, who simultaneously received another sword from Alathos. He pivoted to face Raphael. "If I asked you to distinguish between the soul and the spirit, could you?"

A look of consternation crossed Raphael's eyes as he responded, "I could try."

Rayeh chuckled, "That will not be necessary, but if it were possible, 'Taan,'" and he looked down at the sword, "is that sharp, that precise. Be very careful with her."

A look of puzzlement flashed across Raphael's face. *"Her?"* he thought.

Rayeh chuckled again, "Never mind, just be careful," and he handed him the sword.

"Should I unsheath her?" He said "her" with hesitation.

"Only in dire circumstances, in the utmost need."

Raphael stood to weave her beneath the cord around his waist and step back into the semi-circle.

"Uriel." They all heard a light tinkling in the air as Alathos intoned his name. While all the archangels appeared related, something about Uriel distinguished him. Perhaps it was a clearness of purpose, a singleness of vision, an innate innocence. Can you have something purer than pure? If you could, that would be Uriel. He stepped toward Rayeh and took one knee.

Rayeh had retrieved the sword from Alathos and now presented it to Uriel. "This is 'Boker' Dawn, the first light," Rayeh spoke just above a whisper. "Lucifer received Helel, the bright star, but this is dawn. One day you will understand how unique this sword truly is, how truly special."

Uriel nodded his thanks, but was beyond words. As he slowly stood to withdraw Boker from its sheath, darkness and awe covered them all. The sword began to lightly glow, dispelling the darkness, increasing in intensity until it seemed they all stood in full daylight once again. Uriel sheathed the sword and stepped back into the semi-circle.

"Raziel," was called forward by Alathos' command. Before he stepped out of the semi-circle, he loosened the cord that tied his robe about his waist and tied it around his neck.

R'gal thought, *"What?"*

Haniel leaned over to him and flatly whispered, "He's often like that."

Raziel stepped forward and took a knee.

Rayeh reached behind his back and when he returned his hand to his front, he held a gem between his thumb and forefinger. He began, as Raziel's eyes widened, "Mysteries can be wonderful. They also can be distracting. You must be careful to discern which is which." Rayeh turned around to receive the sword from Alathos. He swung back around with flourish and held it out to Raziel, who had retied the cord about his waist. Before he gave the sword to him, he drew the blade. The air was filled with a note of purest beauty that drove Raziel to his other knee. "This is 'Oz,' a revelation of Glory. Only a few of the seven match this blade." He reversed the blade and handed it pommel first to Raziel's one hand, the scabbard to the other. Raziel struggled from his knees to take the sword and scabbard. He held the sword aloft at arm's length and basked in its glory for just a minute, then gracefully sheathed it and wove it into the belt around his waist. He stepped confidently back into the semi-circle.

"Haniel, it's your turn." Haniel stepped forward and stood there looking at Rayeh's back, who had turned to Alathos to receive the next sword. As Rayeh turned around, he began spinning the sheathed sword between his two hands like he would a staff. It must have been firmly in its scabbard so as not to come out with the force of the spinning. Haniel intently watched Rayeh's hands spinning the sword and at exactly the right moment he reached in to take over the spinning without interruption. Then during the spin, he executed a movement that placed the scabbard between the rope and his robe, only to draw out the sword as he began to weave arcs in the morning air to the purest of music. "Haniel, you have received 'Hane,' which means Favor." Rayeh pointed towards the moving sword, "May he always sing for you like this!" After another incredible arc cutting the air, the sword found its way into the scabbard and the music faded. Haniel was hardly winded and smiling from ear to ear.

As the last note's echo ceased, R'gal, unbidden, knelt on both his knees before Rayeh, his head bowed. Rayeh stepped toward R'gal, turned R'gal's head to the right with his hands and pulled it to his chest, embracing him. It was almost embarrassing in its tenderness and intimacy. Alathos lifted the last sword out of the cart and held it out to Rayeh over the cart. Rayeh reached back for the hilt of the sword with his right hand, still holding R'gal's head to his chest with the left. Alathos placed the hilt of the sword in Rayeh's hand. Rayeh removed the sword, and swung it around to in front himself, between them, with its tip pointing to the ground. "You, my friend, are my right hand. This is 'Yaman,' also my right hand. May you both ever stand before and beside me, in the place none other can inhabit."

R'gal leaned back out of Rayeh's arms, grasped the sword to his chest, and wept openly. Rayeh fully re-embraced him and the sword, and they both wept. The moment was so sacred that first Gabriel, then all of the angels, turned away to give them this moment in private. Then the portal that Lucifer had gone through reopened and music unimagined until now poured forth. They all drew their swords and joined their voices as the cosmos engulfed itself in praise. Then they walked together through the portal.

Chapter Four
Training

The seven of them emerged out of another forest into a field of more close-cropped grass. On the left stood a long bench with what appeared to be eight piles of clothing. Behind the bench stood nine poles, each about four cubits tall. Out of each pole protruded two metal hooks. On the one closest to them hung a sword and a robe and at the near end of the bench sat a very fit man in the bloom of his prime. He stood as they approached.

"My name is Rayeh," and he chuckled familiarly.

Gabriel looked confused, but spoke first, "Rayeh is a young boy. We left him and Alathos over there," and he motioned back into the forest with a head nod.

His smile was infectious, "Sometimes I am and yet I am here." He gestured to himself with both hands. Barefoot, dressed in linen breeches that came to his mid-thigh, he had a wooden sword strapped to his hip. "You may hang your swords and robes on the posts and then dress as I am." While not loud, his voice exuded the authority of command.

Another portal opened about fifteen cubits into the field and Lucifer came stumbling out of it. He gained a stable stance as he looked around, "Why am I here?" he growled.

Rayeh gestured to the pile of clothing and pole nearest himself and repeated his instructions, "You may hang your sword and robe on the post and then dress as I am." Lucifer humphed at being told what to do, yet complied to the obvious authority of Rayeh's command. The others already were doing the same. As they all finished dressing and strapping on their wooden swords, Rayeh continued, "You have each been gifted a sword, but you are unaccustomed to them. They must become a natural extension of you." He pointed to a lone tree at the end of the field about four stadia away. "Run, touch that tree, and return." Most of them looked at each other before they realized they had given R'gal a head start. Off they tore, running like the wind.

Lucifer smiled slyly, turned into his winged form, and was about to launch himself into the sky when he was stopped with, "Lucifer, in your human form!" He frowned at Rayeh and took off at a run in his now human form. Dead last by twenty-five cubits, he only got about a dozen strides, before his sword tangled in his legs, tripped him, and he fell headlong onto the grass. He struggled to his feet and looked ahead, glad none of the others had witnessed the debacle. He began again, this time more carefully. Rayeh shook his head. He had seen Lucifer's fall. Why did it seem like it foreshadowed something else?

They were all pretty evenly matched, although Gabriel and Michael had closed some distance between themselves and R'gal. R'gal touched the tree, turned for the return run and almost collided with Gabriel, who had removed his sword to reach out, touch the tree, and gain precious seconds on R'gal. Michael did not use his sword and now found himself in third place. He wondered if there were a prize for being the first one to complete the task. He suddenly found resources within himself that until now he had been unaware existed. He brought them all into play and quickened his pace, beginning to close the gap.

Rayeh still stood near their starting point, but now further out in the field. He had another pole in his hand. "The first one to touch the pole!" he called out. Gabriel, R'gal, and Michael were running at full tilt, neck and neck. R'gal held out his right hand to Gabriel, his left to Michael. They both quickly, each, glanced at R'gal's hand. Michael somehow drew his sword out with his left hand, while Gabriel drew his out with his right. They joined hands with R'gal, reached out their swords, and touched the pole as a trio. They laughingly turned around to watch the rest of them touch the pole, some with their hand, some with a drawn sword.

Lastly came Lucifer. He looked at Rayeh, then at them all and smiled. This time it was genuine. "Best two out of three?" They all laughed, embraced, and beat one another on the back. The exhilaration of the race and the completion of the task had been something new for them all.

"So, what did you learn from this task?" Rayeh queried.

Haniel answered, "There's more to us than meets the eye?"

"What do you mean?"

He continued, "I mean, I think we are all more or less equal, even though Lucifer came late to the run." The others laughed and Lucifer pointed at Haniel menacingly, then also laughed. "But when Michael, R'gal, and Gabriel joined hands there at the end, I felt something wonderful stir in my spirit. They became somehow 'more'!"

"Ah…" Rayeh almost sang, "a very important lesson. We are always better together."

"Lucifer?"

"The others didn't see me trip over my sword as I began running, but the mishap drew on reserves in me that I didn't know existed. I almost caught up to Haniel, although that's not a very great accomplishment." Haniel pointed menacingly back at Lucifer, then he also laughed.

Rayeh began again, "Although we are currently in a physical world in human form, it is still as equally about the spiritual as it is about the physical. We must not let the physical become a limitation. Come with me."

A portal had opened between Rayeh and the benches. They walked through as a group and found themselves in a large work area.

"This is one of Alathos' work rooms." They could hear a banging and clanging going on somewhere nearby. "He forged the swords you were each given, but he is much more than a smithy. I will simply say, 'He is a master.'" Rayeh sat down at a small round table. There were gears and pulleys beneath it connecting to two pedals on which Rayeh now placed his feet. He began to push one then the other in rapid succession and the round table began to spin. He reached over and took a handful of something. "This is clay, a special kind of earth, mixed with water." He dipped his hands in more water. "And this is a potter's wheel." He cupped his wet hands around the spinning wet clay. The clay began to take shape. When it was round, he pushed in the center with one hand while lifting up from the outside with the other. It began to look like a bowl. He stopped and pointed to his left. "Over there is an oven, a kiln. We could bake the clay in it and it would become hard. Paint it with glaze and fire it again in the kiln and it would become a bowl we could use for eating and drinking." He threw his bowl back into the pile of clay. "Alathos has had more practice at this than I have, but that will suffice for this lesson. Now, back to the field."

The portal reopened and they all stepped back onto the training field. "First I need to teach you a new way of sitting.

Kneel." They all knelt around him. "Now, sit back between your ankles." They did, then all looked at one another. "I know, it doesn't look very comfortable, but it actually is, isn't it?" They nodded. Rayeh jumped back up to his feet in one fluid movement. "You can try that later," and he smiled. "There are a number of words for 'circle.' I am only going to use two of them right now. Geel means to spin, like in a dance. Zeer means to spin in a circle and form, like the clay on the potter's wheel. So, 'Zeergeel' would be to form or create something while spinning like in a dance. Let me demonstrate."

His feet were spread shoulder distance apart, his right foot a half span forward of the left. "Here are the first five movements of the initial form." As his left hand moved to grip where his sword was attached to his belt, he pivoted his right shoulder forward and down. His right hand removed the sword as he took a step to the right, the sword continuing in one fluid cut to the front, and up to the right where he called out at the top of the arc, "One!" Rotating his hand as he proceeded to slash downward towards his left leg, while taking a step backward with his left foot, pivoting to expose his right shoulder and exclaim, "Two!" His left hand joining the sword, he swung the sword backwards in an arc moving upwards, as he stepped back with the right foot to face forward again calling, "Three," at the top of the arc. He slashed down in front of himself, "Four," pulling the sword back to his abdomen and thrust straight forward, "Five. Here it is again. One, two, three, four, five." He resheathed his sword into his belt, "Now, your turn."

They all leapt to their feet, all except Haniel, who rolled backwards, pushed off with his hands and flipped up onto his feet all without getting tangled in his sword.

"Form a line in front of me and spread out a little." He looked at them. "Spread out a little bit more. Okay, now slowly, watching closely. Begin. One," and they approximated his movements. "Two," and they continued to follow, "Three, four, and five." He smiled, "Good, you're all quick learners. Return your swords to your belts. Now again, and I will just watch. Begin, one…two…three…four…and five." They were quick learners. Already they performed it nearly flawlessly. "Again, one…two…three…four…and five." They continued three more repetitions and then began speeding it up faster and faster, until their wooden swords began to sing. Finally, Rayeh stopped them, "Time for some refreshments," and a familiar portal opened to show their robes and swords hanging on the poles. "Change back into your robes and I will meet you at the refreshment table." Rayeh walked through the portal. It remained open, humming as it hovered there just above the grass, until they had all put their robes on over their breeches, and walked back through the portal as a group.

Chapter Five
More Training

The table had been replenished with chilled wine and fresh fruit. They took their usual places, all except Lucifer, who after stepping through the portal, turned around to face where they had just been.

Haniel called out to him, "If you're hoping there will be anything left you better hurry up and join us."

R'gal held out a deep purple fruit to Raphael, "You want to try one now?"

He smiled, shaking his head back and forth, "They're still too sweet to be healthy." He grabbed a dark green one, took a bite and held it out towards R'gal. "This is more like it." He took another bite.

Rayeh stood near Lucifer. He had returned to his young boy form. Lucifer finally reclined at the table. R'gal held the deep purple fruit out to Rayeh. "Is this really too sweet to be healthy?"

Rayeh seemed to contemplate his answer before he spoke. "In a world where everything is good, can something be more good or less good? That is an interesting question. If there is good, is there also not good?" He looked around at all of them. Lucifer seemed puzzled, but Rayeh addressed Gabriel, "What do you think?"

He pondered a moment before he answered, "If I can run faster than Raziel, does that mean Raziel's running is less good? Must we all be the same for us all to be good? We all look similar, like we are part of the same family, although Lucifer is perhaps 'special-er,'" Lucifer pointed at him shaking his head, "but we are not all identical. Part of the beauty of 'goodness' is variety."

Rayeh reached up to caress his chin and nod in assent, "That is a good," he paused, "answer," he chuckled. He looked down at Lucifer whose brows were still furrowed. "To compare and contrast is not to find fault or blame, but to elucidate differences and identify the aspects of variety, just as Gabriel, Michael, and R'gal's joining hands to finish the race together complimented their abilities." While still somewhat befuddled, Lucifer began to nod his assent also. "Enjoy your respite and then join me back on the training field." As Rayeh strode off across the hill towards a low-hanging cloud, he called back, "R'gal, try the green one Raphael is eating." Rayeh entered the cloud.

R'gal reached out his hand to Raphael who handed him the last bite of the green fruit. He tried it. Not as sweet as the purple one, but every bit as good. He mouthed a "thank you" to Raphael. They spent a few more minutes in friendly banter, then rose from the table.

R'gal posed the question, "Who do you suppose is cleaning up after us? Maybe we should at least stack the plates and cups at one end of the table."

Lucifer shrugged, but the rest took their cups and plates to the end of the table. They had just finished doing so when another portal opened and three men walked through it carrying trays, wet washcloths, and towels. "Are you tasked with washing and cleaning up after us?" R'gal asked.

The foremost of them looked at him almost reverently, "Yes, sir."

"Well," R'gal stumbled over the words, "Thank you."

"It is our pleasure to serve, sir," was the reply. The others joined in thanking the men. The man winked, "And thank you for collecting the dishes at this end of the table for us."

R'gal winked back, smiling broadly, "You're welcome."

The three of them set their trays down. Two of them began washing and wiping down the table, as the third moved the dishes and cups to the trays. The archangels' attention was diverted by the opening of the portal back to the training field. The eight men passed through the portal, removed their robes, and joined the adult Rayeh again.

"Did my teaching sword movements in a set of five seem to work okay?" He seemed to genuinely want their opinion. There was a general nodding of heads. "Great! Then here are the next five," and he demonstrated them. Then he again worked with them, watched them, and had them speed them up. "Now let's add these five to the first five." They did and practiced until they performed all ten smoothly and rapidly. "Now backwards." They looked at him with brows furrowed. "Just kidding," he laughed. He added five more and when they had all fifteen memorized, five more. They now each had all twenty movements in their repertoire.

Rayeh began, "I can see some of, well at least one of you, is getting a little cocky because you know twenty sword movements and feel you can execute them flawlessly. I won't mention any names." They all looked at one another, but it was Gabriel who blushed. "Okay big guy, come on up here. I have taught you twenty offensive movements, but what about defensive ones? You start the twenty I have taught you."

Gabriel was no longer blushing, "How fast?"

Rayeh replied, "As fast as you like."

"Do you want me to count them out?"

"Nope!"

Gabriel's hand went to his sword as did Rayeh's. He began at about two-thirds speed until his sword reached the top of the arc, where he joined it with his other hand, only to find his sword meeting Rayeh's with a resounding "crack!"

"Now what are you going to do? You can't just stop in the middle of a sword fight." Gabriel looked bewildered. "You would normally complete the arc and swing your sword down past your left leg as you pivoted around the left, but the arc has been thwarted. So, you pull your sword back to the left, without finishing the arc, and pivot around to the left. Do that!" When he came back to the front there was another "crack," but this time Gabriel expected it. He recovered quickly to pull his sword back and then thrust forward, although Rayeh diverted the thrust from Gabriel's sword towards his chest by pushing it past him to his right. He addressed them all, "Each time the movement is thwarted by the opposition, there is a way to modify or reverse the movement, and guide it into the next one." Back to Gabriel, "Continue with the rest of the twenty movements." At each "crack" it took a moment for Gabriel to perceive his way out of the conflict and back into the next movement, but he got quicker until all twenty movements were completed. He was breathing heavily from both the physical and mental exertion as they finished. Rayeh nodded his approval. "Take Michael and go through the movements together with him."

Rayeh looked at Raphael, "Next." This continued until they each had a partner and they were practicing together. Rayeh addressed them all. "As you become more confident, speed up the movements until you are all sparring at full speed."

Soon the air was filled with "crack" after "crack" and the sizzling and whooshing of wooden swords flying through the air. Rayeh stood off to the side, again nodding his approval at the progress they were all making. He finally stopped them with a, "Good, very good. I will meet you at the refreshment table shortly."

Chapter Six
Teaching the Others

They donned their robes again over their breeches and stepped back through the portal to the refreshment table. It had been restocked, this time with a number of different kinds of fruits and raw vegetables.

Raziel ventured a question to them all, "What do you suppose initiates and controls the portals?"

Rayeh stepped out in front of them through another portal, "That's a good question. The short answer would be knowledge and need. The long answer we will cover another time." He turned from Raziel to address them all, "It is said that the best way to learn something is to teach it. So, just as I taught you the first five movements, you will teach the others. Then the next five until they have learned all twenty. Then dismiss them for a brief respite and meet me back here. Oh, you may take a fruit with you if you'd like, I'll be back for each of you in just a moment. Lucifer," and he motioned him towards the portal.

Lucifer grabbed a bright yellow fruit and joined Rayeh as he stepped back through the portal which closed behind them, only to open again, a moment later. "Gabriel!" Rayeh called out. Gabriel followed Rayeh back through the portal, fruit in hand. "Michael, you're next!" Then it was, "Haniel." Haniel stepped up to the portal, turned, smiled, waved comically, and then turned back around to step through the portal. This continued until R'gal reclined at the table by himself. The portal opened and Rayeh stepped out. R'gal began to scramble to his feet, but Rayeh held up a hand, "It's okay, just a minute." He stepped to the table, poured himself a goblet of wine and sat on the edge of the table. He took a long drink. "Let me tell you what you will find on the other side of the portal. I might as well tell you now while we're here and I can get a drink of this, too. I feel like Gabriel, too much talking." He grinned, just a little. "Over there, I will introduce you to ten…well, let's call them 'commanders of one hundred,' angels, and you will teach them the sword movements as I taught you. The first five, until they can do them nearly flawlessly and quickly, then the next five, and so on until they have mastered all twenty. I know I am repeating myself, but," he looked at the goblet, "this is quite refreshing. Then you will dismiss them to teach ten of their hundred and meet me back here. Okay?" R'gal nodded. "Let's go."

The assembled commanders stood at attention when R'gal stepped through the portal. Rayeh spoke first. "This is R'gal, your archangel. You will find him a capable teacher. You will like him, respect him, grow to love and revere him." Rayeh turned his back on them, winked at R'gal and stepped back through the portal.

R'gal looked the ten angels over slowly. Their appearances were more varied than that of the seven archangels. These could have been part of a number of related or extended families. They were all about two finger-widths shorter than he was.

"What are your names?" Initially surprised that he didn't speak to them in more of an authoritarian tone, they realized that they were actually pleased and as Rayeh had predicted, they began to like him. They introduced themselves one by one and in an orderly manner. "Is one of you considered to be your spokesman?"

Addar spoke up, "Meraiah thinks he is." A chuckle ran through the group and Meraiah frowned.

R'gal turned to Meraiah, "You are all able to assume your winged form?" Meraiah did and was quickly followed by the rest. They were all about a half a span shorter than R'gal's height if he had assumed his winged form, "and back?" Just like that, they were human again. R'gal pointed to a bench on their left with ten piles of clothing, in front of ten poles on which they could hang their robes. "I would appreciate it if you each donned trousers, girded yourselves with a wooden sword, and we will begin to learn one of my currently favorite pastimes, swordplay." They chatted amicably among themselves as they did as he requested. R'gal began again, "Are you familiar with the process a potter uses to form a clay bowl?" He taught them about circles and then began his lesson on swordplay. When complete, all ten of his commanders could flawlessly and rapidly perform all twenty of the movements.

A portal opened. It almost seemed like the portals had a mind of their own. They always opened at the right moment and gave access to the right place. R'gal and his ten commanders stepped through to a refreshment table prepared for them, to experience informal conversation that bonded them even closer. Then they returned to their training field.

R'gal was quite pleased with their progress and they all felt his admiration. "You have mastered the initial offensive swordplay movements. Now it is time to learn the defensive ones. Meraiah," and he motioned for Meraiah to stand opposite him. "Begin the first five movements."

"At what speed, sir?"

"You choose, but remember I am going to be demonstrating the defense to your offense." Meraiah began at about two-thirds speed and as he got to the top of his first arc, he met R'gal's sword with a resounding "crack". "Your arc has been thwarted from proceeding around and down to your left leg, but you can bounce your sword off that meeting of swords, down to your left leg, and continue the movement." Meraiah came around to another "crack" at the top of his arc, pulled back, thrust forward, and would have skewered R'gal in the gut if R'gal hadn't pushed Meraiah's sword off to the left. R'gal continued, "At each place your movement is thwarted, you must discern how to regain the movement, and move on into the next one. Meraiah, let's go through it one more time," and they did.

"Now, Meraiah, you teach the defensive moves to Addar." Meraiah proved as adept a teacher as he had been a learner. They proceeded through the movements a number of times and soon they were both ready to begin again. "Meraiah and Addar, each choose a partner and teach them." The whole process was a wonder to behold. "Now the four of you each choose a new partner. Begin again." That only left two commanders, Tilon and Shamah. "Tilon and Shamah," R'gal chuckled softly, "I'm going to see how closely you have been paying attention. I want you to teach each other." Although they both looked surprised, they realized this was a very special opportunity and both rose to the occasion. In a short time, they were sparring flawlessly. The rest of the commanders actually applauded them as they finished. Smiling, they both turned to face R'gal.

R'gal motioned for Shamah to come to him. R'gal moved his sword on his belt around to his right hip. Shamah's jaw dropped as R'gal whispered, "Let's see how adaptable you are in the reverse." Shamah quickly moved his own sword to his right hip as R'gal commanded, "Begin," and drew his sword with his left hand. Shamah was only a heartbeat behind him and recovered quickly to meet him: crack, whir, crack, whir, crack, until they finished all of the twenty movements in the reverse.

Shamah's eyes were wide with a mixture of awe and excitement at what had just happened. He had performed flawlessly a set of movements he had never actually learned. R'gal threaded his sword through his belt, moved it back to the left, and led all of the others in cheering "Bravo!" followed by applause for Shamah's demonstration of adaptability. The others all joined in showing their appreciation of Shamah's accomplishment.

Chapter Seven
Swordsmanship to All

R'gal's words were expressed with deep appreciation, "There is time for a short respite and then I will meet you again." R'gal stepped through one portal and another opened for the commanders. They found the table newly prepared for them and began discussing the experience they had all just shared. It seemed like not nearly enough time had elapsed before another portal opened and R'gal reappeared. He stepped to the table and retrieved a fruit while ten portals opened around them. "Each of you commanders is to return through a portal to find ten of your angels ready to learn what you have just learned. Then you will teach another ten, and another, until your entire hundred is fluent and flawless in the use of the wooden sword."

Addar, the first to step towards his portal, turned back to address R'gal and the rest of them, "Why are we learning to use the sword?"

R'gal responded, "There are many things you need to learn in order to become the incredible beings you are meant to be. Swordsmanship is one of them. That will have to suffice for the time being." Addar nodded his acceptance of R'gal's answer, turned to face the portal and stepped through.

R'gal then stepped through his own portal and was back at the archangel's table of refreshments. The others were already reclined, eating, drinking, and comparing experiences. Rayeh stepped through his portal right behind R'gal.

"Gentlemen," they were, after all, in their human forms, "I want to take a few minutes to debrief your experiences in teaching your commanders of a hundred and I would like R'gal to go first."

"Is that because he showed up last?" Haniel needled.

"Ah, yes, 'the last shall be first,' that is an important principal, but no, that is not the reason. Go ahead, R'gal."

"I don't think we did anything that special. After introductions between us I spoke to them about the potter's wheel, the two circles, then taught them the first five movements. I taught them the next five which they added to the first five, and practiced a few times until they were all doing it very well. Then we added five more, then we added the final five and practiced until they had all twenty moves memorized. We went back to the refreshment table for a short respite." He took a quick drink from his goblet. "Then we moved back to the practice field and I paired up with their apparent, recognized spokesman." He looked at Gabriel. "I taught him the defensive movements much like we had learned. I had him teach one of the other commanders, then those two taught two more, and all four of those taught four more. That left only two who hadn't learned the defensive moves. I had those two pair up and teach each other to see if they'd been paying attention. They had! They did splendidly. I figured that I had completed my task, but no portal opened.

So, as I waited, I had an interesting thought. I called one of the last commanders that had learned to come forward. I moved my sword to my other hip, the right, and said, 'Let's see how adaptable you are in the reverse. Begin!' As I drew my sword with my left hand, he quickly moved his sword to his right hip and followed suit, drawing it with his left hand. He was able to flawlessly perform the movements against me in reverse without ever having learned them. It was wonderful to behold."

There was a hushed silence. It felt almost holy. Raphael finally broke the silence by stammering, "You...taught them... the movements...leading with the left hand?"

R'gal smiled in the midst of the admiration he rightly deserved, "Yes, and it was amazing and beautiful."

Haniel followed up, slowly, "No wonder he was the last of us to arrive. Did any of the rest of you teach your commanders leading with the left hand?" They all shook their head.

Rayeh prodded, "What have you learned from R'gal's experience in teaching his commanders the left-handed movements?"

Gabriel stood slowly and seemed reluctant to look Rayeh in the eyes. "We are not just to follow commands to the letter, but we should be willing to actively go beyond them in seeking to please you and Chayeem." The others added their "Yes," one by one, each standing to do so.

Lucifer stood last. "How do we know what more we should do, when we have only been asked to do a particular task?"

"Chayeem knows your heart. If you desire to do more, he will aid you. He speaks to each of you separately as well as when you are together."

It seemed so simple, yet Lucifer still seemed perplexed. He nodded anyway, then smiled awkwardly at the others asking, "Shall we head back to our commanders and teach them the left-handed movements?"

They nodded as portals opened for each of them except for R'gal and Rayeh.

Rayeh's smile to R'gal was not awkward, "Thank you for that spontaneous 'extra'. Feel free to have a few moments to yourself while I go have a chat with Chayeem." A portal opened for Rayeh and he stepped through. R'gal filled a goblet and walked around to his normal position at the table.

Chapter Eight
Celebration

The portal opened before the pillar of fire. Rayeh stepped out of the portal and into the pillar. It always seemed more spacious inside the pillar than it looked like it could be from the outside, an observation not lost on Rayeh.

The Tree spoke to him, “Have they figured out who you are?”

Rayeh looked at his feet as he smiled, “I don’t think so. They just know that I speak with the authority of your voice.”

“I know that this must be difficult for you, to be limited by time and space. I appreciate that you have chosen to do this.” There was deep affection in every syllable of every word that the Tree spoke to him.

“It is my pleasure.” He now looked directly at the Tree. “What’s next?”

“Before we go there, I would appreciate your observations, your opinions. What do you think of my servants, the angels?”

“How much time do we have?”

"That is a rhetorical question," the Tree chuckled, "because you know that time here really doesn't matter. So, what do you think?"

"Well," Rayeh seemed to ponder for a moment, "they are pretty incredible. It's not like you were just practicing on the way to creating something else." He smiled, "There are many things about them that are the same: size, shape, color, and yet they are all somewhat different. I think that one of the things I really like about them is their variety. Some are funny, some more serious, they have a capacity for joy and initiative. Take R'gal, he was teaching his commanders of a hundred the initial twenty moves with the wooden sword that he had been taught. Then he had them teach each other the defensive moves, all this similar to the way I had taught him, while leading them with the right hand. Then, on his own, he sparred with one of his commanders, doing the whole twenty moves while leading with his left hand. It was truly amazing, especially that his commander was able to spar in the reverse just as easily!"

"Yes," commented the Tree, "I really did enjoy that. What do you think of my establishing them in a hierarchy?"

Rayeh again seemed to ponder. "It does seem to lend itself to an efficiency in the dissemination of commands. However, I wonder if, in the long run, it might prove to cause them to rely too much on the external structure rather than on their direct communication with you personally."

"An interesting point. You don't think we can have them operating one way personally and another way militarily?"

Rayeh's voice got very serious, "What will happen when they are told one thing by their leaders and they think they have received something else from you personally?"

"Hmmm, how could that even happen?"

"I'm not sure it can or will, I'm just trying to explore all the options."

"I guess that is why I asked you," the Tree chuckled, "isn't it?"

Rayeh smiled in return, "Yes, I believe it is."

"Well then, we should plan for all contingencies." The Tree paused, "Back to your original question about what's next. I was thinking that once all the angels have mastered the initial twenty sword moves...."

The seven archangels had taught their ten commanders of one hundred lieutenants. Then each of those one hundred lieutenants taught their fifty captains of fifty sergeants. The captains then taught their fifty sergeants of thirty squad leaders and each sergeant had taught their thirty squad leaders of ten. Once the squad leaders had completed teaching their angels, a total of five and one quarter billion angels knew the twenty basic sword movements. These angels now stood on the plains that surrounded the hill where the One Tree currently stood in all of his splendor.

Rayeh stood before the Tree and spoke, his voice projecting so all could hear him, even those who stood at his back. To make them all feel equally welcome, he circled the Tree as he spoke. Still, they each heard him as if he stood next to them, speaking as a friend.

"Welcome! You have all learned the twenty sword movements both in offense and defense and have performed them to the satisfaction, joy, and sometimes even to the amazement of your leaders, but this is the first time you have all assembled before Chayeem to display them for him as one body."

The seven archangels surrounded the tree. Each of their ten commanders arrayed before them. Spread out before the commanders were their one hundred lieutenants, fifty captains, each with fifty sergeants with their thirty squad leaders of ten. A vast ocean of angels covered the plain below the Tree standing majestically on the hill.

"Lucifer will lead us in a song of worship. I will take Lucifer's place among the archangels as we perform the twenty movements accompanying his worship. After having seen how the movements are performed in worship you are all invited to join in as we do them a second time as he repeats the song. Lucifer?" Rayeh and Lucifer traded places.

Lucifer took a deep breath, sounding the opening note of his symphony, and thus he began with the archangels to accompany him.

We are his angels of power and mystery,
Serving before the Great Tree of majesty.
We will fulfill his every command,
Acting as both his voice and his hand.
Nothing he wants will remain undone,
We are one, we are one, yes, we are all one!

The music, the words and the singing swords put together all so powerfully reverberated in every heart that it had been nearly impossible for the rest of the angels to just stand there watching. They gasped in relief when Rayeh addressed them, "Now, you may join us!" The entire cosmos groaned in ecstasy at the beauty of an ocean of angels worshipping before the Tree.

"Bravo!" The word from the Tree sounded deeply in their ears and hearts.

Rayeh turned back towards the Tree, "There is more," and turned back toward the angels. "Return to your areas of respite and your leaders will exchange your wooden swords for ones of the finest metal and craftsmanship. Then pick a partner to spar with and return to accompany the words of the second verse."

Portals seemed to open everywhere, but they were all and each one at the right place. The angels seemed to disappear as they walked through the portals, only to appear moments later wearing new swords in ornate sheaths, paired up, and ready to spar with each other. Another hush of holy silence enveloped the entire sea of angels. Lucifer inhaled again preparing for his opening note.

His every desire (clang) and wish we fulfill (clang),
Enforcing his edicts (clang), desires, and his will (clang).
Beholding his power (clang), beauty, and might (clang),
The darkness withdraws (clang), encountering his light (clang).
The cosmos rejoices (clang), it has all understood (clang),
He is good (clang), he is good (clang), all things are good.

The clatter of the angels simultaneously banging their swords together side on side against their neighbor's thundered like a chorus of wondrous applause. Then all the leaders turned from facing their angels to face the Tree and the entire sea of them sheathed their swords and took a knee as one before the Tree.

The words again sounded in their ears and their hearts, "Well done!" The satisfaction that filled his voice brought tears to all the angels' eyes. "You may now return to your areas of respite and receive your assignments," and the portals reopened. The angels slowly rose from their knees, seeming almost reluctant to leave the wonder of this united spectacle. Finally, they turned, walked through their respective portals and disappeared, leaving only the Tree and Rayeh.

Rayeh turned to the Tree smiling, “That went well.”

Back came the Tree’s chuckled response, “You expected anything less?”

PART TWO

A World Too

Chapter Nine
In My Garden

He had created a garden. In its middle grew an orchard, and in the middle of that rested the stones of fire. They were the colors of ruby, topaz, and diamond; of peridot, onyx, and amber; of sapphire, aquamarine, and emerald; of amethyst, garnet, and zircon; and two other stones that defied description. In the midst of the stones walked an angelic being, singular in his beauty. An intricate network of golden pipes and precious stones covered him. His every breath created a symphony of unimaginably beautiful music with lights flashing in unison with it. Sometimes the music and the brilliance of the stones seemed to rival that of the origin of light itself, overshadowing everything that there was and all that it seemed there ever could be. The angels would join him to form a choir of praise that it was by his nature to produce and perform. He was the choir director, choreographer, and conductor of the worship of the cosmos. He was called Lucifer by his brothers and he wielded the singing sword Helel, the brightness of the morning star.

One day Rayeh walked through the middle of the garden, to stop before the stones of fire, and listen to Lucifer's latest masterpiece. As always, the lights and music mesmerized. As Lucifer paused between movements of his symphony Rayeh stepped forward, laid a hand on his shoulder and said, "Chayeem has decided to create another race of beings. He will create them in his own image and likeness. Let me show you a vision of what he intends. Perhaps you can compose something worthy of them, his finest creation." Rayeh showed Lucifer the plan that Chayeem had birthed in his heart. Lucifer bowed deeply, and Rayeh exited leaving him to the task.

Lucifer was confused and somewhat troubled. He thought of himself as the pinnacle of Chayeem's creative genius, but now there was to be something more? Could it be possible that there could be anyone or anything more beautiful and wonderful than himself? For the first time in his life, he began to doubt the wisdom of Chayeem. He reached down and gripped the pipes that surrounded his heart. He gripped them so fiercely that he actually bent and distorted them. He found that he could now produce different notes and chords. The harmony of the cosmos began suddenly to tilt on its axis.

Lucifer went to Alathos concerning the damage he had caused. He wondered if his symmetry and balance could be restored. While it was not beyond Alathos' skill to do so, Lucifer found himself unable to endure the pain required to complete the repair. Lucifer decided that he would rather live with it as it was. Soon, it no longer bothered him. He cautiously added the new notes into his compositions in such a way that no one appeared to notice. It seemed he was only expressing the uniqueness of his identity. There was, after all, no one like Lucifer. He was the zenith of worship, the covering of the entire garden, expressed from amidst the stones of fire.

Alathos stood before the Tree. "You know what has happened to Lucifer?"

The Tree responded melodiously, "I do."

"He is opening up new realms of music." Alathos was worried.

"There is no one else like him in all of creation. Why does this bother you?" Chayeem prodded.

"It seems less like worship and more like he is pushing a personal agenda." There, he had said it!

"Hmmm, it is different. The universe has never heard anything like this before."

Alathos took what seemed to him to be the next step, "You're sure that this is good?"

Suddenly Rayeh stood at his side. "Could I show you something?"

It was interesting that his appearance, though unexpected, had not been startling. "Certainly."

"Do you mind if I ride?"

"Of course not, I would be privileged…" but before Alathos could complete the sentence, Rayeh was on his back, a portal opening before them.

Rayeh, smiled and pointed at the portal, "Onward, to the new world!"

They walked through it to emerge out of a forest, into a grass covered meadow, much like when R'gal had joined them. Yet this one had a feeling of even more pristine innocence and smelled divinely new. Rayeh slipped from Alathos' back. Before them stood a small patch of dirt. Rayeh knelt on both knees, reached forward, cupped his hands, and scooped up two handfuls of dirt. "This is earth," he let the dirt slip through his fingers, "this whole place is called earth, and this ground is holy."

Alathos was already on all four of his knees kneeling next to the patch of dirt. "Yes, I can feel the sacredness of this place."

"Do you know why Lucifer altered himself?"

Alathos questioned, "You mean the pipes around his heart?"

"Yes. It was because I showed him a vision of this," and he took the two handfuls of the dirt, spat into it and began to mold it, make it into a form that resembled an angel in its human form. "Could you help me? Just reach out your arms to cradle his upper body as I set him on the dirt." Alathos did as Rayeh demonstrated, moving forward as Rayeh lifted the upper torso of the form, head and shoulders, to rest in Alathos' arms. Rayeh stood up and walked around the figure whose upper body was now cradled in Alathos' arms. "Hmm, I've never done this before, but here goes." He straddled the form and knelt down to look at him straight in the face. He leaned over, tilted his head a little to the side, and covered the form's mouth and nose with his own mouth. He breathed into the form's nostrils the breath of life and man became a living soul.

His chest expanded just as Rayeh removed his mouth. The man's eyes opened, and he smiled, "Hello."

"Hello, Adam," Rayeh said as he stood and offered Adam a hand up to help him also to stand, not that he needed the help. It was more a gesture of friendship than assistance. Alathos had also stood, although Adam had not even acknowledged that the centaur was there. He seemed to only have eyes for Rayeh. Rayeh shifted their hand grip and they began to walk, hand in hand, towards the edge of the forest. Rayeh called back over his shoulder, "Be right back." Adam did not seem to realize Rayeh had even spoken to Alathos. He was mesmerized by Rayeh and the forest.

"*What a splendid place,*" Adam thought. They walked a short distance through the forest to another smaller meadow with a bench.

Rayeh motioned to the bench, "Could you wait for me here," he pointed to the bench, "I shouldn't be long."

"Sure," and he released Rayeh's hand to sit on the bench. Off to the right ran a small brook. Adam folded his hands and looked contentedly towards the brook.

Rayeh turned silently and walked back to Alathos who stood there waiting in a state of awe.

"When I completed my first singing sword, there was a sense of holy satisfaction, of doing what I was made for, but this," Alathos pointed towards the forest where Rayeh had left the man somewhere.

Rayeh finished his sentence for him, "Your swords are 'good,' but this is good with a capital 'G.'"

"Yes! It nearly takes my breath away," added Alathos.

"That is what has troubled Lucifer. He knew that Chayeem had made him good, but then I showed him very good. Now we have to wait and see what Lucifer will do with this new knowledge."

Alathos whispered, "What he has already done perplexes me."

Chapter Ten
Discord and Discontent

It isn't fair!" Lucifer thought, "It just isn't fair! Why would he create someone else? He has all the angels! He has me! Why would he need anyone else?" His breathing was uneven and ragged. He tried to calm himself and found that he couldn't. He started to compose;

Full of strength and majesty the Great Creator stood
With but a word he made all things and then pro nounced them good.
The first to shine, bright morning star no other showed such splendor
Eternal beings formed of light their glorious praises render.
What being formed of dust and mud could ever thus displace us?
More than created, creators we
Eyes fresh open, now we see
To rule, not serve, our destiny
My shattered soul embraces.

He quickly crumpled the parchment and dropped it amidst the stones of fire where he stood. He couldn't believe he had actually penned the words. A tune had even come to mind. As the parchment became cinders, the tune still haunted him. This tasted odd, almost of betrayal. He had to be very careful, but he still had difficulty focusing. He quickly penned something else, but it lacked the luster of true worship. It felt forced, contrived. His heart was not in it. He tried again with a similar result. What should he do? Should he ask for help? In whom could he confide? No one! It would be a sign of weakness. He regulated his breathing. Control returned slowly, though it seemed somewhat tenuous. He wrote again. He found that he could camouflage most of his feelings, but with the passage of time more and more often the feelings invaded his songs. He seemed to be opening up entirely new realms of expression, better, fuller, more honest. He felt like he was finally proving his potential, entering into the fullness of all he would become.

Most of the angels quit listening and participating in what used to be Lucifer's leading of worship for it seemed like it had become something else. However, some of the angels remained, entranced by Lucifer's new thing. They had never heard anything like it. It stirred them deeply, and they found themselves agreeing with it at an elemental level. They could not deny that they had each been created glorious beyond compare!

Later, Lucifer and two of the archangels gathered around the table. Lucifer lounged at the head, Haniel on his right, Raziel on his left. There were goblets of wine and a pitcher on the table, nothing else. It seemed a bit spartan for Lucifer's normal opulent ways, but then he seemed in a dour mood.

Haniel ratcheted up his courage until he could speak, "Your music seems to have taken a turn in a different direction recently. What's going on?"

Lucifer looked like he'd been slapped, "Do you have any idea what Rayeh is planning?"

Raziel hesitantly asked, "He hasn't told us anything. Has he said something to you?"

"He showed me, he actually showed me." He sounded nearly maniacal.

"What did he show you, Lucifer?" Haniel whispered.

The mention of his name seemed to bring him back to his senses a little, "He is going to create another race of beings. To replace us."

Haniel and Raziel looked at each other, puzzled, "To what?"

"They will rule the planet earth instead of us." He was winding himself up again. "We help him rule everywhere else, why not on earth too?"

"Why would he do that? Have we done something wrong?" Raziel seemed confused, shaking his head from side to side to dispel the mist enveloping his mind.

"You're sure you saw this?" Haniel questioned. The look he received in return dispelled all doubt.

"He told me and then showed it to me in a vision. He even asked me to compose a symphony in their honor. He said they would be made in his image." Rayeh's saying that had seemed to make things worse.

"Does that imply that we aren't?"

"He called them, 'My finest creation.'" Speaking to himself Lucifer continued, "I thought I was his finest creation, and now he's going to displace me?" It didn't seem possible, especially to Lucifer.

Haniel tried again, "And there's no possibility you misinterpreted his intention?"

He got that look again, "None!" Lucifer nearly shouted.

Raziel squeaked out, "Should we try and do something? Maybe he told you expressly to see how you would react?"

Lucifer pondered that a moment and then quickly dismissed it. "The vision left no room for comment or debate. It was obviously a finalized decision and he was overjoyed at sharing it with me." Lucifer got up from the table. "I wanted you to know," and he summarily dismissed them. As they walked away Lucifer pondered, *"Is there really something or someone MORE than me? Does that mean I am less than the best that I could be? How can 'I' become the MORE? Perhaps I need to seize this chance? Yes! That's it, this is my opportunity to become..."* and he left the statement unfinished.

As Haniel walked away he wondered, *"Should I go and talk to Rayeh myself?"* However, he hesitated to sidestep Lucifer's authority. To go around him might be a total disaster. Still, something needed to be done.

Later, Haniel was sparring with Zadok, one of his commanders, when he suddenly found himself disarmed.

Zadok seemed as shocked as Haniel, "My lord, you're not yourself today."

Haniel shook his head to dispel the cobwebs, "Yes, an obvious example of how not paying full attention to the task at hand can put you in harm's way. Let's take a break for a few moments." They sheathed their practice swords and walked to the refreshment table.

Zadok poured Haniel a drink and handed it to him. "Anything I can help with, my lord?" Zadok was unquestioningly his finest warrior and, as he had just demonstrated, nearly his equal.

Haniel wondered, *"Can you be promoted to the position of archangel or must you be created as such? Hmm, an interest-*

ing question." He turned back to Zadok. "I'll be back in just a bit," and walked off across the training ground.

A portal opened and Rayeh stood on the other side beckoning him to walk through it. He did and they stood in the middle of a dense forest that Haniel didn't recognize. "You have some questions," Rayeh smiled. He did that a lot.

"Yes, I do," Haniel confided.

"Go ahead, ask away." Rayeh always seemed so calm, so relaxed.

"Well, for starters, can an angel be appointed to the position of archangel?" There, that was easier than he thought it would be.

"Like Zadok, for instance?" Rayeh's smile deepened.

"If you knew my question already, why do I need to ask it?" It did seem almost redundant.

"If you handed me a purple fruit and said, 'Taste this, it's almost too sweet,' not knowing I had already tasted it, would it be redundant for me to taste it for your benefit?" Sometimes he spoke in riddles. "Or for efficiency's sake should I just admit that you are right?"

Hamiel shrugged his shoulders, not knowing where this was heading.

"Tasting the fruit you offered me would enhance our relationship more than the efficiency of my just agreeing you were right. Don't you think?" Haniel thought about it and then nodded his assent. "In a similar manner, just because I know you have a question doesn't negate the benefit to us both of allowing you to ask it."

"Okay, thanks for letting me ask it." Haniel spelled it out. It did seem to enhance their relationship.

It was Rayeh's turn again. "And I have a question for you. Would you be willing to split your ranks in half and give one half of them to Zadok if he were to be promoted to archangel?"

That stopped Haniel for a moment, then he replied, "Can I get back to you on that?"

Rayeh chuckled, "Certainly. What else can I help you with?"

Haniel took a deep breath. "Lucifer seems to be struggling with something. It is affecting his worship, maybe even his leadership."

Rayeh looked down a path that headed left and off into the distance. "Yes, he is trying to work through some things. I would think it would be easier if he just came and talked to me, but you know how independent he likes to think he is. Your support will be a big help to him, if he will let you."

"So, you know what's going on?" Haniel acted surprised, yet realized he was not, not really.

"Yes." Rayeh simply answered.

"And you already know the outcome?" Haniel was trying to grapple with things he still didn't understand.

"Just because I know the destination doesn't necessarily make the journey any easier." And for some reason Rayeh looked at the ground.

"And you think that I can help Lucifer?"

"If he will listen to you, most definitely." Rayeh looked Haniel in the eyes.

As Haniel looked back at Rayeh, "And will he listen to me?" Rayeh raised his eyebrows, but didn't answer the question. Haniel continued, "and do I have your blessing?"

Rayeh nodded once as he said, "Yes, you do." The portal reopened and Haniel stepped through it and back to his own place in the heavens.

Lucifer's lyrics wandered astray more each day. They seemed to be sequential steps in an entropy that played out before everyone who was still listening. He finally expressed the topics of his doubt in the present situation and the beginnings of what he saw as a way forward. He placed before them the seeds that they, the angels, might be able to create a better heaven. Most of Lucifer's followers soaked up all of his ruminations indiscriminately, but Haniel found his loyalties challenged daily. Rayeh had suggested that he could help Lucifer work through things, but what if Lucifer's schemes turned to complete revolt? Haniel found himself severely conflicted at every turn.

One bright star shown in the darkened skies. Zadok continued to demonstrate all of the qualities and characteristics that exemplified an archangel. One day while the two of them sat on the banks of the river, Haniel felt the impulse to broach the topic.

"Zadok, what would you think of becoming an archangel?" Haniel postulated.

Nearly struck dumb, Zadok stammered, "Is that even possible?"

"I mentioned it to Rayeh and he didn't dismiss the idea. In fact, he asked if I would be willing to part with half of the angels that report to me in order to give them to you."

"And you said?" Zadok left the question hanging while looking at the ground.

"I told him that I would get back to him," Haniel replied to the bowed head. "That's why we are having this little discussion." And they left it at that.

The portion of heaven that included Haniel and Raziel's armies and those angels from the others archangels who were joining Lucifer directly from the influence of Lucifer's compositions, continued to coalesce into a distinct and separate force within heaven. Raziel would follow Lucifer anywhere, regardless of the consequences. Haniel still tried to make sense what was happening, but all to no avail. The momentum was building. Soon there would be no hope of redirecting what was moving towards open revolt. Haniel had hoped he could be of some use in the situation, but was feeling more and more like a pawn in a game that was out of his personal control.

Lucifer called a counsel. It seemed a counsel of war and that worried Haniel in no uncertain terms. There were only the four of them: Lucifer, Haniel, Raziel and Balar, the main commander of the forces that directly allied themselves under Lucifer. It was rumored that Lucifer had promoted him to the rank of archangel and that he had even given Balar his own sword as a symbol of his rank. Balar obviously thought of himself as equal to Haniel and Raziel. Haniel could tell that Balar's delusion of Lucifer's grandeur matched Raziel's. Of Balar's leadership skills and fighting prowess Haniel had no first-hand experience.

Alathos stepped through the portal to address the Tree. Rayeh stood next to it, one hand fondly on the trunk. Alathos bowed and spoke haltingly, "Can…we…do…nothing? Will you do nothing? Lucifer moves towards revolt, not even trying to hide it anymore."

"You think this has escaped my notice?" The Tree's words hung heavy, laden with sadness.

"No, I'm sorry! I was impertinent." Alathos still hung his head.

"No, you are worried, but all will be well." It seemed there might still be hope. "How many of the angels follow him?"

"Rumor has it that Raziel does and all his angels. Even Haniel seems distracted and that worries me most. I would conservatively estimate it at about one-third of the angels." Alathos spoke matter-of-factly.

"And?"

"I fear there will soon be war." The sadness deepened.

“And you think I can avert all-out war by....?” Rayeh left the question hanging.

“By acting quickly and decisively.” There, he had said it. He sighed deeply.

A portal suddenly opened before Alathos and the Tree. R’gal stumbled backward through it, a sword protruding through his chest, his own sword falling to the ground, then his body.

Lucifer, in his winged form, stepped through the portal, stooping towards R’gal’s sword, “I have bested him. I am taking what is rightfully mine!”

Alathos sprang toward R’gal’s sword, grabbing it first, forcing Lucifer to pull his own sword from R’gal’s chest instead. Alathos cried defiantly, “No!” With the full force of an angel verses a centaur the two swords met. The impact was cataclysmic, the sound both beautiful and horrific. Beyond them, through the portal, Chayeem could see the battle waging for right to rule heaven.

Suddenly Rayeh was astride Alathos as he knocked Lucifer unconscious. Alathos grabbed Lucifer by the throat of his breastplate as he started to fall. Lucifer’s sword clattered to the ground and was trampled underfoot as Althos unceremoniously dragged Lucifer back through the portal where Rayeh’s word of command echoed through the cosmos. “Enough!”

The fighting stopped. Alathos let Lucifer’s body fall to the ground, picked up Lucifer’s sword, and threw it across his still form.

“Begone!” and Rayeh had barely spoken the word when Lucifer, Raziel, Haniel, Balar and all their angels winked out of existence in the realm of heaven.

Chapter Eleven
Another Garden

Adam sat quietly on the bench, listening to the brook, watching the light sparkle on the water, when he heard someone coming. He turned to see Rayeh enter the meadow. "Back so soon? I must admit this is a wonderful place." Adam was sincere, but speaking almost childlike. He probably wasn't used to speaking at all yet.

"As promised," Rayeh held out a hand. "Shall we?"

Adam took Rayeh's offered hand and together they walked out of the glade in a direction different from the way they had entered. There wasn't a lot of light filtering through the trees, but it was more than enough for them to see the pathway they followed.

Unexpectedly Adam stopped and looked to his right. "*This tree is different,*" he thought and the word "*oak*" sprang into his mind. "Is that an oak?" he asked Rayeh.

"Why, yes, it is." Rayeh seemed pleased that he would know.

They continued to follow the path until they turned a corner and it opened into a beautiful orchard. All manner of trees grew there, of variety innumerable, bearing fruit of different kinds. Adam was initially struck speechless, but finally exclaimed, "Wow! This is even more wonderful than the meadow and the brook."

Rayeh let go of his hand to spread his arms indicating it all. "I have made all of this for you, Adam."

"For me, really?"

"Yes, for you." They continued to walk through the orchard. Rayeh picked a fruit from one of the trees, one for himself and one for Adam. He bit into his, then handed Adam the other one. "Try this."

He tasted it. "Wow! I think my favorite word is going to be, WOW!" and he laughed.

They came to the center of the garden. Two trees stood there. Rayeh pointed to the white one. "That is Chayeem, the Tree of Life." He pointed to the other one. It was difficult to look at for some reason, like it wasn't fully present. Rayeh pointed to it. "That is the Tree of Knowledge. You may eat of any of the trees in the garden except that one," and he pointed to the Tree of Knowledge. "The day you eat of it you will begin to die."

Adam wasn't sure what Rayeh meant, "you will begin to die," but it was obviously not something to be desired. So, all he said was, "Okay."

They continued to explore the garden for the rest of the day, occasionally trying a new fruit. When they got to the deep purple one, Adam exclaimed, "Hmm, that's almost too sweet, but still good." As dusk darkened the garden, they found a spot under an oak where the grass was close-cropped and soft.

Adam smiled, "I have a question."

Rayeh returned the smile, "Ask away."

"Why are you wearing," the word "robe" popped into his mind, "a robe and I am not?"

"Do you feel the need to wear a robe?" Rayeh chuckled.

"No, it's just a question."

"I feel comfortable wearing one, but I can take it off if you'd rather."

"No, that's okay, I just wondered."

Rayeh sat down with his back to the tree, Adam beside him. "It's going to get dark. This is what we call night and it is a time for you to sleep. I think you will enjoy it. Here, you can lay your head in my lap." Adam lay on his back with his head resting on Rayeh's leg. "Close your eyes, I'll sing you a song, and when you open them again, it will be morning."

Walking thru a garden, eating from an orchard
What is more delightful than being with a friend.
Seeing all the beauty that is set before you
Hoping it will never, never ever have to end.
But the light it dwindles, soon it will be twilight
Time to rest and close your eyes, to embrace the night.
Yet you know, you surely know, tomorrow's light will come
And you will be united, wholly and completely with your friend.

Rayeh looked down and Adam was asleep.

Chapter Twelve
Awakening

R'gal's eyes blinked open, his mind still a little fuzzy. He sat with his back propped up on something soft and warm. Two arms were wrapped around him. He turned his head around to look over his right shoulder.

Rayeh smiled at him tentatively. He had been cradling him in his arms. "You've had a difficult time. What do you remember?"

"Lucifer and his angels attacked…the Tree!" Panic engulfed R'gal. "Is he okay?"

"Yes, we're all okay. You defended us valiantly, but were slain. Alathos knocked Lucifer unconscious, dragged him back through the portal he had opened, and I stopped the revolt." The sadness in Rayeh's voice brought tears to R'gal's eyes.

A look of shock and dismay suddenly washed over R'gal's face. "I was slain?"

"Yes, Lucifer thrust his sword clean through your chest and then pushed you through the portal he opened. I think he hoped its shock value could be used to his advantage." The picture was pretty grim, even stated factually.

R'gal placed his hand on his sternum. "But… I feel fine."

"You may be slain, but not destroyed. You are immortal." There was a twinkle in Rayeh's eye.

R'gal pondered that for a minute. "I am… immortal!" He'd never thought about it before. As the thought settled, he asked, "But you stopped the revolt...?" and left the sentence unfinished.

"And banished Lucifer, Raziel, Haniel, and their angels from heaven." The repercussions of that pronouncement were catastrophic.

"And now what?" R'gal queried.

Rayeh smiled, "How much time have you got?" It was becoming his favorite line. R'gal shrugged his shoulders. "The short answer is, while not inevitable, we were prepared for Lucifer's revolt. We have planned for all contingencies. We are simply implementing some of those plans now." He paused, "I made a new garden and planted it on earth where I have given it into the hands of a new guardian, the man made after my image, and placed a new angel, Uriel, to cover it." He paused again.

"I do not know 'the man,' of which you speak, but Uriel performs everything with noble efficiency." R'gal spoke with reverence.

"Yes, he does, doesn't he. But what about you? You have not asked of my plans for you." Rayeh teased him gently.

"I'm sure you will tell me what I need to know when the time is right," he said trustingly.

"Well, for starters, your sword, Yaman, was lost in the conflict. You are now an archangel without a singing sword." The tinge of sadness had returned to his voice.

"Yes, there is that." R'gal now felt the loss acutely, though unable to put it into words.

"You don't need to put it into words," Rayeh read his thoughts. "I can feel your pain and loss quite fully." It was the epitome of empathy, Rayeh's knowing without having to be told.

R'gal looked down at the empty scabbard. "I don't know if losing a limb could feel any worse. I keep looking down, expecting him to be there. I can still feel his weight on my hip. I want to draw him, just to hear him sing. What is this feeling?"

"It is called grief, something else new in our world, a world which used to be entirely good." After a pause, Rayeh's smile returned, "I do have some good news though. Alathos is forging you a new sword. I don't know how long it will take, but then time, eh?"

"I don't know if I can bear someone else in my hand, we were so fit for each other."

"As true as that was, it is no longer," Rayeh consoled. "Think of it as turning a page, a new chapter."

"And my position in front of the Tree?"

"Ah, another change," he added almost off-handedly. "The Tree now resides in the garden that has been transplanted to earth. So, it has the man and Uriel to guard and protect it. I want you to try something new for me."

R'gal suddenly began to feel hope, not pain for the past, but hope for the future. A new sword, a new something else?

"Are you ready?" R'gal thought it might be a rhetorical question. Rayeh continued, "You know how when you say 'wings' in your spirit, you change into your winged form?" R'gal nodded. "I want you to say 'horse' and change into a horse."

"I can do that?" R'gal sounded unconvinced.

"Sure, do it," urged Rayeh.

R'gal took a slow deep breath and said "horse" in his spirit. There, before Rayeh, stood a majestic black stallion that could have been Alathos' twin, except for the man part of the centaur. It was a rather odd feeling being four footed, but not completely unnatural.

Rayeh laughed, "Walk around a bit and get used to yourself." He did. After a moment a portal opened. "Through we go," and together they walked through the portal to the original training field with the tree in the distance. "I'll race you to the tree," and off he went. Rayeh was rather quick. R'gal took a few more tentative steps and then broke into a gallop. He won, but not easily. Rayeh smiled, "Mind if I ride on your back? You'll need practice at that too." R'gal nodded. Rayeh grabbed a handful of mane and vaulted aboard. "Start off slowly." He did. "Try a trot," that went fine too. "Cantor," he went a little faster. "Now… a full gallop!" R'gal broke into full stride. He found it nearly as exhilarating as flying, and he nearly did fly over the ground. He forgot all of his previous grief for the sheer joy of his hoofs pounding the ground and the wind whipping through his mane. Then he remembered Rayeh was on his back, but it didn't matter, they flew as though they were one. Finally, he slowed down into a walk, then stopped, and Rayeh slipped off his back to hug his neck. He slowly brushed his hand down R'gal's nose. "I really enjoyed that. Thank you!"

"Thank you!" R'gal found he could still talk. He wasn't sure why it surprised him.

"Ready for another assignment?" Rayeh chuckled.

"I get to turn into something else?"

"No, this is enough for now." Rayeh chuckled more heartily. A portal opened before them. They stepped through and into a meadow in the middle of a beautiful forest. There stood the most beautiful light brown mare, as majestic in her own way as R'gal was as a stallion. "R'gal, this is Soosa."

He was awestruck, dumbstruck, just plain struck speechless. Finally, he nodded in greeting, "Soosa, my pleasure."

"Mine too," she replied. Why was he surprised again, that she could speak too. He guessed it was because she was someone, something, he'd never met before.

"Excuse us for just a moment, Soosa," and Rayeh led R'gal out of earshot.

"She's...a...a...." He didn't have a word for it.

"She's a mare, a female horse." Rayeh filled in the blank.

"A what?"

"Oh dear, how to explain 'female' in thirty words or less." Now that was an interesting task. Rayeh began, "You angels are all the same. There is no female counterpart for an angel. That's why when you appear in your human form you do so as males. In this new creation everything has its counterpart. You appear as a male horse; she is a female horse. She is everything about a horse that you are not. Together you make the species, the idea, the meaning of horse, complete."

"So, she's not an angel appearing in the form of a horse?"

"No, she's a real horse, part of this new creation."

"Ok," R'gal said, "I think I get it," but it still didn't sound like he really fully understood. "Can you tell me why she smells so good? I just want to go over and nuzzle her."

This was going to be harder than it seemed. "That's fine, just don't get too carried away. Chat with her for a while until I call you, and then come through that opening in the woods over there," and Rayeh pointed.

A portal opened and with a bemused look back at the two horses Rayeh stepped through it.

R'gal walked over to the mare, "So, Soosa, what can you tell me about yourself?" and he took in a deep breath of her scent.

Chapter Thirteen
The Naming

Adam had rolled onto his side and was still asleep in the grass. His arm cradled his head as he lay beneath the oak. Rayeh sat down beside him. He reached over, ruffled his hair tenderly and whispered his name, "Good morning, Adam."

He yawned, "That was interesting. I get to do that every night?"

Rayeh smiled, "Grab a fruit and let's take a walk." It was more suggestion than command.

Adam smiled, stood up, grabbed a deep purple fruit. "Yes, let's." He bit into it, scrunched up his face. "It's still pretty sweet," then smiled even more broadly, "but still good."

They walked up a small hill to crest it and be engulfed in an incredible view. "Wow!" That word again. "I think this is the most wonderful of all." Just off to the left was an opening into the forest. Before them, at the bottom of the hill, a short level lawn flowed to the edge of the great river that wandered through the garden. It was a stunning scene.

"So far? Yes." Rayeh sat on the crest of the hill and patted a spot beside him.

"This was made for me too?" Adam spoke hesitantly as he sat beside him.

"Yes, I have made this entire world for you. Everything and everyone will cooperate with you fully," Rayeh shared, admittedly proud of his work.

"Everyone?" Adam questioned.

"Ah, that is next. I have brought you here to introduce you to the animals of the field and the birds of the air. Whatever you call them, that will be their name." Silently Rayeh called for R'gal.

R'gal walked together with Soosa out of the forest, regal majesty personified. Adam gasped with a short intake of breath. "Horse?" it was more than a question.

R'gal bowed, bending one knee and leaning forward, "Yes, sir. That is who I am, and her name," the pronoun seemed odd, "is Soosa. She too is a horse."

Adam seemed intrigued, "You are the same, yet different?"

Rayeh stepped in, "Together they are horse. He is a male and she a female. They complement one another, complete one another."

Soosa bent a knee as she stepped forward and bowed, "A pleasure to meet you, my lord." Adam seemed unperturbed that they both talked. He had no reason to expect differently. He got to his feet as they approached to nuzzle him on each shoulder. He put his hand around, under their necks, to scratch them both under the ear. He heard something behind him as the two horses walked away.

"There are more." Adam turned back to look again at the forest opening as a lion and lioness emerged.

Adam said firmly, "Lion!"

"Yes," responded Rayeh, "and she would be called a 'lioness,' the female version of a lion." He had a great shaggy mane and, of course, she did not. They knelt on one knee and said in harmony, "My lord." Adam stepped between them to scratch them behind the ears. They gracefully padded past him as he turned again to the forest, to be astounded once more.

"Grrrraffe," and he burst out laughing.

Rayeh queried back, "You're kidding."

"You said whatever I called them. Well, maybe 'giraffe' will be their name, but the grrrr was in response to their long necks." They brought their heads down together to intone, "My lord," and he kissed them each on their foreheads.

The next pair came, loping out of the forest on their hind legs, the knuckles of their hands connecting with the ground every few lopes. The male crashed into Adam, enveloping him in a crushing embrace. "My lord!" he grunted as he nearly squeezed the life out of him. Trying desperately to catch his breath, Adam gasped, "Ape." The female had loped up with the male, but just stood there, embarrassed, probably. When the male released him, Adam reached out a hand, the female responded. Adam took her hand and kissed the back of it. He whispered, "Princess." She looked down as though embarrassed again. He dropped her hand and looked back towards the opening in the forest. They kept it up all day, until animals of every size, shape, and kind filled the entire area below the hill.

Rayeh called out, "R'gal, Soosa," and they galloped over. He looked Soosa in the eye, "May I?"

She nodded and said, "Of course." He grabbed a handful of mane and threw his leg up and over her with the grace of a dancer.

Adam's eyes went wide after that display and he hesitantly said to R'gal, "May I?"

R'gal nickered, "Certainly." Adam grabbed a handful of mane himself, threw his leg up and was surprised the next moment to find himself astride R'gal.

He grinned from ear to ear, "I did it!"

R'gal responded, "Was there ever any doubt?" and nickered again. A portal opened and the four of them walked through it. They found the usual refreshment table, complete with fruit and drink, on the other side, with a short grassy field and small brook for the horses. Adam and Rayeh slid off the horses and left them to the pasture. Adam reclined at the table.

"I have a few questions," he inquired. Rayeh nodded. "If you and I are the only men here, who prepared this table?"

Rayeh smiled his infectious smile, "I thought you were going to ask me why everybody refers to you as 'Lord.'"

"That's my next question." He too was smiling, questioningly.

"The simple answer to the second question I have already mentioned. This was all made for you. They are too. You are to benevolently rule them and all of this." He spread his arms about him.

"And the table?"

"There are others to serve you that you haven't met." Rayeh paused, "What do you think is the purpose of today?"

Adam pondered before answering gravely, "I have met many today whom I like and will grow to love, but none of them is my counterpart."

"Yes, you are very perceptive, but we aren't done. We still have the birds of the air," and he winked at Adam.

After a few more moments of refreshment, they called the horses back to them, remounted, and rode back through a portal to name all the birds. Yet there was still not found one who was fit to become Adam's helper and counterpart.

Chapter Fourteen
A Deep Sleep

Mentally exhausted, Adam lay down on his back in the grass, his head resting on the interlocked fingers of his hands. Rayeh sat next to him, his arms wrapped around his knees, "We still found no counterpart for you, no helper fit to labor beside you."

Adam felt an emptiness in his heart. He whispered, "No, we didn't."

"Go to sleep and I will take care of it." Adam closed his eyes and fell asleep, in a deep, deep sleep. While he was asleep Rayeh took a rib from next to his heart and fashioned it into a woman. When he was finished fashioning her, the pinnacle of all of creation, he closed up the wound from which she was taken and woke the man.

Adam's response can hardly be put into words. This was not just some 'other' bird or animal. This was all of the image of Chayeem that he, Adam, was not. Adam said, "This one is of my very bone, she is part of my very flesh. I will call her 'Dawn' for she is the beginning of all things bright and beautiful." And he embraced her and felt whole, complete, like he had finally found home.

Rayeh blessed them and said to them, "I want you to go into all of the earth and fill it with wonder. I want you to take leadership of the earth to rule, guard, and protect it. I have given every plant with its seed and every tree with its fruit to be food for you, for the beasts of the field, for birds of the air, for every creature in which there is the breath of life." And Rayeh pronounced, "This is all very good."

One day Dawn walked through the garden assembling breakfast from the produce of all of the trees. About to walk by the Tree of Knowledge that stood in the middle of the Garden next to the Tree of Life, she noticed someone perched in its branches. Lucifer, the craftiest, most subtle of all the creatures was awestruck at the perfection of the beauty of Dawn. Everything on earth had its counterpart. He and the fallen angels had none, yet here was a woman worthy of himself. He determined to have her. Combined together they would create a race that would rule the world and the heavens.

He spoke and his words radiated an unknown power, "I see that you are gathering fruit for your meal. Here, have one of mine," and he offered her a fruit from the Tree of Knowledge.

Entranced by his words she responded tentatively, "We have been told that we are allowed to eat of any tree in the garden with the exception of this one," and she pointed to the Tree in which he lounged. She scrunched up her face "I don't think we are even supposed to touch it."

Lucifer laughed and it sent shivers down her spine, "No? Why does he withhold it from you?" and he laughed more boldly. "Because he knows that eating from my Tree will bring you enlightenment. You will be as full of light and knowledge as I am. You will be as full of it as he is himself. That is why he has forbidden you." He extended the fruit again. It seemed to glow with a light all of its own. As she looked at it, she felt the desire for it within her rise up. She took it. Nothing happened. She turned it over and over in her hands. It truly was a wonder and did appear to emit some kind of light she had been denied. She bit into it to feel an intense feeling that she had never experienced before. She turned from the tree. Adam stood next to her. She extended the fruit to him, its pungent aroma extending to encapsulate him as its juices dripped from her mouth and hands onto the garden floor.

Time stood still. Adam had a choice to make. Join her or lose her to this forbidden experience. Slowly another thought began to dawn deep in his soul. What if there were another way? What if there were a law greater than the one stated, one deeper, more powerful than the one she had just transgressed? What if he offered his own life to pay for Dawn's wrong? Could he fulfill the requirement of the broken law with the sacrifice of his own life? But then Dawn would be alone in the world. Who would guard and protect her? No! He could not leave Dawn to face an uncertain future alone. He chose to be with her even in this. He grabbed the fruit, took a bite, and his eyes too were opened. He realized they were naked, and he was ashamed. He held out his hand to her. She reluctantly took it and they walked past the Tree of Life. On the other side of it grew a fig tree. They took some leaves from the fig tree to cover their nakedness. Later, they wove the fig leaves into aprons to cover their nakedness more permanently.

That afternoon they saw Rayeh walking among the trees of the garden, and they hid themselves.

Rayeh appeared to be looking for them. Finally, he called, "Adam, where are you?"

Adam answered, "I saw you walking among the trees, but I hid myself."

Rayeh questioned, "Why did you hide yourself?"

Adam looked down at the fig leaves woven about himself in an attempt to hide his nakedness, "I was ashamed."

Sadly, Rayeh asked, "Have you eaten of the Tree of Knowledge?"

Adam hung his head deeper in shame, "Yes." He looked at Dawn, "She gave me some of its fruit. There seemed no other way for us to remain together, so I ate it."

Seemingly stunned, Rayeh whispered to Dawn, "Do you have any idea what you have done?"

She tried shift the blame, "The man in the tree said that if I ate the fruit that I would become as wise as you."

Rayeh spoke a single word, "And?" He paused, and she looked at the ground, secretly wishing it would swallow her up.

Lucifer dropped out of the tree, smiling. Rayeh's words, though barely above a whisper, echoed throughout the cosmos. "Because you have done this THING, you are cursed over all that is created. This begins the war between you and the woman's offspring. One day you will think you have him at your disposal, but he will crush you." Lucifer crumpled to the ground, writhing, and crawled painfully out of the garden.

Rayeh turned again towards Dawn, "You will bring forth your children in pain. It will dampen the joy of their birth, and you will be subordinate to the rule of your husband, tarnished as his complement."

Then he addressed Adam, "You have chosen to step outside of my desire. Forgetting that I know best, you have taken things into your own hand. Therefore, the ground will no longer cooperate with you, but fight against you. You will toil and labor unsuccessfully to bring it back under control. Your food will be the result of the sweat of your toil until you return to the ground, for you will return to dirt."

The animals had gathered and witnessed Rayeh's words. Two lambs stepped forward and bowed, offering, "We will cover man's guilt and shame." The five of them then walked back to the middle of the garden. There, before the Tree of Knowledge, the man and the woman each placed a hand on the head of a lamb, and the two lambs laid down their lives for the man and the woman. Rayeh fashioned garments from their skins to clothe the man and the woman.

A portal opened and a man stepped out of it. Rayeh spoke to him gently, "R'gal, will you please escort them out of the garden." R'gal reached out a hand to each of them, which they took, and he ushered them out of the Eastern Gate down a path that led to where they did not know. When the two of them looked back at the gate, two majestic winged beings now guarded the entrance, each holding a sword of mysterious flame, blocking the way to the garden. When they turned back around R'gal had disappeared and they were alone.

Rayeh called the two angels, Zach and Jephi. "I want you to follow Adam and Dawn, to guard and protect them, but I do not want them to know who you are."

Zach smiled, excited by the prospect. "We could appear as animals."

Rayeh also smiled, intrigued by Zach's idea. "And what would you become?"

"The first animal Adam ever met was a stallion," he ventured.

Rayeh addressed Jephi, "and for Dawn?"

"A gazelle," replied Jephi.

Rayeh chuckled, "That will work, catch them quickly."

The two angels transformed into the animals and leapt and galloped out the Eastern Gate after Adam and Dawn until they caught up with them. When Adam and Dawn questioned the animals as to why they had been banished from the garden, they were astonished to learn, "We were not banished. We didn't want you to be alone, so we have come to be with you."

Adam put his arm around Zach's neck, buried his face in it, and wept. Tears filled Dawn's eyes also as she stroked Jephi's head. Then the four of them continued to travel eastward.

PART THREE
His Secret Weapon

Chapter Fifteen
Another Sword

R'gal returned from ushering Adam and Dawn out of the garden. The cherubim nodded as he passed. Rayeh stood a short distance inside the gate and addressed R'gal, "Chayeem is waiting for us." He turned, R'gal stepped up next to him, and they walked to the Tree in the center of the garden. R'gal was puzzled. The Tree of Knowledge no longer stood next to Chayeem. Where it had been, a small apple tree now grew. "It outlived its usefulness," Rayeh said somberly.

Alathos stood proudly next to the Tree, a large smile gracing his face. He addressed Rayeh, "You just completed your finest creation a short while ago, when you made woman." He paused, "I believe I have just finished mine." He had been hiding it behind his back, lying flat. He continued to address Rayeh, "May we present it to him?"

"A few words first," Rayeh interjected. "R'gal, you may be wondering what your part is in things now after having been slain in the revolt. It is more than just turning into a horse on occasion." He smiled, "Although that did allow you to be the first angel to meet Adam. You will find it interesting to know that the angel Zach has taken on a form very similar to yours as a horse, and even now guards and protects Adam in that form. But speaking of your future, there will be a number of assignments that we want you to enact for us in a special capacity. For them you will need a special sword. Therefore, Alathos was commissioned to forge it and it appears that he has completed that task."

Rayeh approached Alathos' flank and stretched out his hands. Alathos placed into Rayeh's hands a sword and a scabbard. A shimmering material wrapped the sword and scabbard and should have made the sword difficult to look at, yet the wrapping somehow enhanced its ability to engage and attract your attention. It was mesmerizingly enchanting. Even Rayeh seemed awestruck and speechless for a moment. When he found his words he murmured, "Yes, Alathos, you have outdone yourself with this one. I will call it 'Shenah' for it embodies change, transformation, your new start, R'gal." He turned, held it out to R'gal, who waited with head bowed, his own hands outstretched, kneeling on both knees. Rayeh placed the sword and scabbard, still wrapped, in R'gal's upturned palms.

R'gal took one slow deep breath, then another. "And what shall I do with this… 'wonder'?"

The Tree, Rayeh, and Alathos responded in chorus, "That which is righteous, noble, pure, and holy."

Chapter Sixteen
The Fallen

Almost one full third of the armies of heaven had participated in the revolt and were cast out of heaven: Lucifer, Raziel, and Haniel, all those who followed them, plus some of those who had reported to the other archangels. They had been banished to earth in their human form, walking around appearing as men.

One of the fallen stood before Haniel now, demanding, "Our Prince summons you!"

Haniel could have chopped him into little pieces, but the fallen angel was only doing as commanded. Haniel buckled on his sword, Hane. "Lead on!" he said abruptly, trying not to include the scorn he felt.

They walked across the finely-manicured gardens, through the courtyard of statues, and into the palace proper with all of its majestic gold trimmings. If nothing else, Lucifer excelled at appearances. There were two large men, the size of himself, blocking the door to Lucifer's throne room. They wore long two-handed swords and held tall intricately carved iron spears. They recognized Haniel and moved apart to let him pass with Lucifer's aide. The throne room too was impressive with its gold filigree highlights, burnished bronze mirrors, and plethora of lighted candles. At the far end, on a dais of ivory and white marble, sat Lucifer on a chair of solid gold. Its arms were bronze lions, and Lucifer's hands usually cupped each head. Off to his right stood a table ornately carved with symbols, filled with nearly raw meats, fruits, and wine. He currently held a bejeweled goblet in his right hand, which a young man stood behind. The man held a large golden pitcher and would top off Lucifer's goblet whenever he held it towards the young man. Just behind his throne on the left stood the palace wizard, complete in dazzling robes and staff adorned with runes, a jewel at its top worth more than the wizard himself. Lucifer didn't need him for his magic. Lucifer created his own. The old man was just for show. Lucifer's aide knelt before the dais while Haniel bowed only slightly in deference.

Lucifer seemed to sneer. He did a lot of that these days. "You're wondering why I summoned you?"

"You needed some comic relief?" Even in these circumstances Haniel retained his humor.

"You think this is funny? No, I am deadly," and he emphasized the word 'deadly,' "serious." Lucifer sat a little taller on his throne. "I have a plan."

Haniel thought to himself, *"I hope it's better than the last one."*

"What?" Lucifer snapped.

"I didn't say anything." Haniel met Lucifer's eyes strongly, boldly, yet without direct challenge.

Lucifer spat out, "I know what you were thinking."

Haniel smiled, "Actually you don't have that ability any longer. That would have been a gift you left in heaven."

"You would defy me?" Lucifer seemed to be building up a head of steam.

"I'm here, aren't I," and he bowed majestically although with comic exaggeration, "my Lord."

"Humph," Lucifer muttered.

"Your plan?"

Lucifer began through furrowed brows, "I have recently returned from the city of men," he said proudly.

"Which one?" Haniel interrupted.

"It doesn't matter," Lucifer continued, "the big one, and we have agreed that in order to cement the union of our two kingdoms they will offer us their daughters. We will become one with them to produce offspring that will forever demonstrate that oneness." He began to whisper, "We will create from these women a race of beings that will rule this planet and some day," he sat taller on his throne, "we will regain the heavens." He wiped some spittle from the corner of his mouth. He sneered, "He thought he would banish me here in human form, but here each species has its compliment. We will take the daughters of men as ours and breed a new race, create a new species." He smiled broadly, but a bit askew.

The thought that came unbidden to Haniel's mind was, *"He's mad, even madder than before the revolt. How can we participate in this foolishness?"* He kept his tongue. Gritting his teeth barely prevented him from screaming out loud. He hoped that this turmoil did not register on his face. Once, Rayeh had asked him to try and help Lucifer work through his confusion. That hope had ended in Lucifer's choice to revolt against heaven. Was there still hope? Wasn't faith hoping when there seemed to be no more hope? And yet now he was as estranged as the rest of the fallen.

"So, what do you think?" asked Lucifer sarcastically.

"Is that a rhetorical question or do you really want an answer?" Haniel hoped only he could hear the mocking in his tone. He dared not say more.

"I want you and Raziel, each of you, to pick twenty, no, make it twenty-one, of your best and send them to me. The daughters of men will be here later today and the two groups will be presented to each other at tonight's celebration. We will have feasting, drinking, and revelry the likes of which we have never seen!" Finished, Lucifer took a long pull from his goblet and then reached it back to be refilled.

Haniel responded neither yay or nay, but simply, "My Lord," bowed slightly, turned and walked out of the throne room.

Lucifer said to himself, "I must have that one watched even closer."

Haniel, on his way to his home outside the palace wall, detoured onto the grounds that belonged to Raziel. Raziel's holdings were much more ostentatious than Haniel's in just about every way imaginable. They were a complex reflection of his mysterious personality. For instance, no direct pathway existed that would take you to the entrance of his home. Rather, obscured by a variety of optical illusions and garden mazes, the path could only be obtained by an esoteric knowledge of the purpose behind each obstacle. In addition, he altered the physical pathway weekly. Fortunately, Haniel knew Raziel well enough to be able to predict each of his latest iterations. He also knew of the hidden guard observation posts and made a few mistakes in the process of getting to the entrance, so as to make their report of his progress obscure his true knowledge and ability.

He suddenly emerged in front of the entrance to greet two of the fallen angels guarding it. "Hashak, Kadaroot, may your path be clearly lit."

"And yours." They both returned to their places after they stepped aside to let him pass. He entered, to be met by a kneeling angel with a basin of water and towel to wash his feet. Haniel knew not where Raziel had uncovered this custom, but he quite liked it. The angel removed his right sandal, washed his foot, dried it, massaged some sweet ointment into it, and placed his foot in a cloth slipper.

"Welcome to the home of Raziel," he half sang as he removed the left sandal to do the same, ending with, "May his house be as yours."

Although not required, Haniel responded, "Thank you." The angel raised his averted head and eyes, smiled, and nodded.

Another angel appeared seemingly from nowhere, "May I take you to him?" Haniel nodded although he could have gone there by himself. It was all a part of the intrigue that Raziel wove around himself like a cloak. Better to play along, he thought. They walked through a short hallway, adorned with interesting hanging art. Raziel was well-traveled and during those travels found the opportunity to acquire the most unusual art, artifacts, and other objects that suited his fancy for the arcane and the mysterious.

Raziel knelt at a low table on which lay an interesting six-stringed box that he was playing. The tune was hauntingly melancholy. Haniel's accompanying angel bowed and excused himself. Haniel stood transfixed, and listened for the longest time. The melody was entrancing, but if the truth were told, Haniel didn't really like it. It was too sad and dark, although captivating.

Raziel stopped, looked up, and realized Haniel stood there. "Oh, Haniel, I didn't hear you come in. What did you think?" and he nodded towards the instrument.

"Hauntingly beautiful, but a little sad for my liking," he shared honestly.

"That's one of the things I like about you, Haniel, you don't pull your punches. I think there's something else, but it escapes me," and he laughed.

"I'm sure it is my bubbling optimism," and Haniel laughed too.

"Remember when life used to be like this, before the revolt?" Raziel mused.

"Yes, sadly, I do remember and it seems so long ago."

"Can I get you something to drink?" A serving angel stood there, pitcher in one hand, goblet in another.

Haniel took the goblet from him, "Thank you," and reclined at the table. "I have news: our Prince's latest plan."

Raziel said it out loud, "Is it better than the last one? It didn't achieve his purpose."

"Hmmm, I'm not sure that this one will either," and he revealed Lucifer's plan to intermingle the race of man with the angels by delivering the daughters of men to some of them, creating a new race to eventually rule the heavens.

After some pondering, Raziel ventured, "And he thinks this will work?"

"He thought the last one would work too, and convinced us to follow him. Some of us followed for obscure reasons, but the resulting banishment we have all tasted."

"Does he want you and I to participate?" Raziel voiced his concern.

"He wants us to choose twenty-one of our best and send them to the palace this afternoon in preparation for tonight's revelry," Haniel explained.

"And you and I?"

"We will need to make at least a token appearance, but I think this is where I draw the line. I don't want to be too obvious though. Although I think he over-estimates his powers, he was once the best of us, except in a footrace." They both chortled over the last comment.

"I have an interesting question for us to ponder," Haniel said with obvious care.

"Yes?"

"Is it possible for us to revolt against the revolt and return to heaven?"

"Who would want to? Here we can do as we please. You must be very careful in speaking of this. I hope you haven't mentioned it to anyone besides me." Raziel was speaking just above a whisper.

"Do you suppose Rayeh still listens to us?" Haniel just lobbed it out there.

"Hmmm, I repeat, you must be very careful. I'm sure Lucifer has spies within our ranks."

"I'm sure he does too. Are you keeping a list?"

Raziel tapped his temple, "Only up here."

Haniel laughed again, "He tried to convince me earlier that he could read my mind. I told him I was pretty sure he left that gift in heaven."

Raziel, "and his response to that?"

A little more somber, "He wasn't very happy with me."

"So, have you picked your twenty-one? Are you one of them?" Raziel queried.

"Yes, I have picked them. No, I am not one of them, but I will at least put in an appearance." Haniel responded, concern written all over his face.

"Ah. Now, can we talk of lighter things?" Raziel hoped to alter the atmosphere, and he played a more uplifting tune on his instrument. Haniel smiled and relaxed.

Chapter Seventeen
The Tree's Council

When the portal opened, Rayeh stood next to the Tree, one arm encircling a lower limb. Through it stepped the remaining archangels: Gabriel, Michael, Raphael, and Uriel, accompanied by the centaur Alathos. They clustered before the Tree as another portal opened and in walked R'gal.

Gabriel greeted him with, "We wondered what had happened after you were slain. Where have you been?" There was deep concern in his voice.

R'gal stepped back from the group and towards Rayeh, "I have been on special assignment."

They looked towards Rayeh, and Gabriel again spoke for them, "Now that R'gal is back, what about his angels, the ones that used to report to him? They have all been reassigned. Should they be assigned back to him?"

Rayeh looked him over. "Those assignments will remain in effect, as R'gal's special work for us will also continue. However," and Rayeh patted the Tree's limb tenderly, "let's move to a less formal location." A portal opened and on the other side they found a table prepared with the usual assortment of fruits and drink.

They each found a spot to recline at the table as Rayeh slowly continued, "Things on earth are gaining momentum in the wrong direction. Lucifer is instigating that wrong direction, one that I am unsure we can avoid."

Gabriel spoke up as usual, "What can it be that you cannot avoid?"

Rayeh slowly looked each of them in the eye as he continued, "The fallen ones are about to join with the daughters of men with the sole intent of producing offspring that will be half man and half divine. He thinks he can thereby create a new race to rule the earth and even regain heaven."

Uriel spoke up, "What?"

Raphael spoke simultaneously, "and you do not believe this thing can be prevented?"

Rayeh almost whispered, "I said unsure, but I would like to try."

R'gal was the last to speak. "Anything! We will do anything that you ask of us." The others all nodded in agreement.

Rayeh sighed deeply in relief. "There is a small chance we might be able to change things. Uriel, I would like you to speak with Lucifer and see if you can dissuade him. Gabriel, I would like you to talk to Raziel, and Raphael, I would like you to meet with Haniel. Michael, I would like you and Althos to remain here and guard the home front."

"And me, lord?" R'gal interjected, his words woven with compassion.

"Let's see how this goes first." He seemed done, but was not. He raised his hand. "The full blessings and authority of Chayeem go with you." Three portals opened, the archangels each took a last pull of the drink in their hand, and stepped through their portal.

R'gal, disappointed, drained his goblet as Rayeh stepped to him and placed a hand on his shoulder. "You are still my secret weapon," he confided.

Lucifer lounged on his golden throne, sipping from his goblet, gloating greatly over the promised results of the night's debauchery, when a portal opened, and Uriel stepped through almost nonchalantly. Lucifer practically leapt from the throne. "What are you doing here? You have no right to be here! Begone!"

Before Lucifer's guards could jump into action, Uriel, still girded with his sword even in his human form, pulled it to produce a note of such purest beauty that the guards fell writhing to the floor. Lucifer, himself, fell back on his throne somewhat disoriented. Uriel spoke, his voice like thunder, "There is no place I do not have the right to be. My rights supersede yours, pretender." Lucifer trembled. Uriel continued, "You must not go through with what you have planned for this evening. It is a great wrong."

Lucifer cackled, "Try and stop me. We have free will; man has free will. Talk to the Tree if you have a problem with that!"

"Yes, but you are not free from the consequences to your actions. There are limits to even his patience," Uriel pleaded.

"Then I will find those limits!" Lucifer sneered.

"I'm sure you will," and Uriel sadly turned away as a return portal opened for him.

Raziel sat in his luxurious garden surrounded by the twenty of his best whom he had personally chosen to participate in this historic evening. A portal opened and Gabriel stepped out before him. Raziel's twenties' hands all went to the hilts of their swords, but Gabriel had already drawn his and its note of clearest purity and power immobilized them all. He addressed Raziel, "I know what you have planned for this evening. You must not do it. You are very close to calling down the wrath of the Tree."

Raziel's smile was a bit askew. "We are making our own way down here. You made your choice. The Tree has lost his control of us. We will do as we please. Leave us alone."

Without a word, Gabriel turned sadly and walked back through the portal that had opened behind him.

Haniel sat alone at a scribe's table pondering what was about to come. He was trying to collect his thoughts and put them onto vellum. Although Lucifer had created his kingdom on earth and was about to unite it with the kingdom of men, things were progressing out of control. Man's rebellion had been about doubting Chayeem and his word. Lucifer's rebellion went deeper than that. He challenged who should rule the universe and he was taking steps to put himself in that place.

A portal opened and there stood Raphael. While surprised, Haniel motioned for him to come through and he did. "Raphael, this is a surprise. What are you doing here?"

A sadness fell upon the room as Raphael walked into it. "I have come to hopefully talk some sense into you concerning tonight and the so-called alliance that Lucifer is trying to forge using the daughters of men."

Haniel looked down at what he had just been writing. "I think it is too late. It has too much momentum already. As you know, the princes of men will all be there offering their daughters to us in order to secure an alliance that will birth Lucifer's new race of beings."

"And what if you stood up in opposition?" pleaded Raphael.

"I think it is too late for that too. I have already assembled my twenty-one participants." He looked out the window at the setting sun. "I must join them soon."

"Must you? Must you join them?" Raphael still held out hope.

"I am not one of the twenty-one, but I must at least make a token appearance. You had better leave before anyone finds out you have been here." Haniel looked back down at the desk and sadly, Raphael returned through the portal.

Chapter Eighteen
R'gal's Next Assignment

Their own portal opened and R'gal could see the Tree on the other side. Rayeh motioned towards it with his head, they both turned, and walked through. Rayeh walked to his normal place beside the Tree and reached up to grasp his favorite branch calling, "R'gal, join me." He motioned towards the Tree. R'gal could not recall ever having actually touched the Tree. As though feeling his hesitation, Rayeh added, "It's okay, R'gal," and he laughed. "He doesn't bite."

R'gal looked up into the branches as he questioned, "Sir?"

The voice that answered him removed all doubt. "I would be pleased if you did." R'gal reached up to hook his hand over a branch. He touched the Tree and his entire being flooded with wonder. Something new and beautiful blossomed in his soul. He stood there breathing slowly, deeply, like inhaling an intoxicating fragrance. Chayeem's voice sang inside of him like his favorite melody. "I'd say, 'Welcome home,' but you were already here. Perhaps you are here more fully now."

"Yes," R'gal smiled, "fully home." He paused, "Rayeh said you had something special for me?"

"As our secret weapon?" the Tree chuckled.

"Yes, there was that too," and R'gal smiled.

The Tree continued, "It nearly broke my heart to banish Lucifer and his rebellion to earth, but to have men so fully welcoming him is even worse. What they have planned will set in motion events that will ripple throughout all of man's time on earth." A sadness replaced the earlier laughter.

"And you think there is a way I might be able to help avert this?" R'gal spoke with some hesitation.

"If I said you are our last hope, would I be stating the case too strongly?" Rayeh interjected as he looked up into the branches of the Tree. He looked back at R'gal, "but no pressure," and he too smiled, then he continued, "One of the princesses of men is going to make a significant impact on Haniel. If you can somehow sideline that, it may be enough to cause a breach in the entire event."

"I will do my best," he replied, although his voice lacked conviction.

Rayeh laughed openly, breaking the tension, "We expect no less."

"Do I need to take anything with me?" His confidence grew slightly.

"Nope, just your winsome personality," and there was more light laughter from Rayeh.

As a portal opened off to R'gal's left, he ventured, "Wish me luck?"

"How about favor?"

"Sure, that would be even better." R'gal turned towards the portal then hesitated and turned back to gesture at the Tree, "and thank you for this…" and further words failed him. Rayeh just nodded. R'gal stepped into the portal.

He emerged in a palace garden. He assumed it was one of the palaces of men. It was beautiful, but for some reason also felt covered with an impending darkness. He turned a corner and it opened onto a small grassy field. Off along the edge sat a young woman on a bench with her back towards R'gal. He cleared his throat as he approached her so as not to startle her. She turned to look over her shoulder. She was ravishing! It stopped R'gal in his tracks. She turned more fully on her bench to face him, "May I help you?"

"I am R'gal, I come from the heavens with a message for the princess." The words just tumbled out. He hoped that was a good thing.

"And you have found your princess. I am Judith." Her smile matched her beauty. "The heavens? What is your message?"

"May I sit?" And she smiled and patted the bench next to her. R'gal heard the echoes of Rayeh's voice clearly in his heart and repeated what he heard. "I know that you are supposed to be meeting with Haniel this evening." Shock crossed her face like a cloud passing over the sun. "He used to be my friend in the heavens, but has come down to earth, and at the moment is not in a very good place."

"What seems to be the problem?" The shock was replaced by concern, perhaps even compassion.

He listened some more. It was a time for only truth. "He was part of a rebellion against the Heavens and was cast down to the earth for his part in it."

The shock returned, "I have met him. He doesn't seem like that at all."

Hmm, more truth. "You probably see him as a wonderful man, but he is not. He is a fallen angel."

Shock began to be replaced by curiosity. "An angel, what is an angel?"

R'gal looked to assure that no one was watching, stood, and suddenly appeared eight cubits tall with wings and all.

Judith almost fell off her bench. She was about to scream when R'gal put his finger to his lips, "Shhhh." She held back the scream, R'gal appeared once again as a man, and sat beside her.

"Haniel is really like that?" and pointed to where he had stood. She obviously fought to regain her composure.

"Yes, but his ability to appear as an angel has been suppressed by his having been banished to this planet."

Back in control she looked at the ground demurely, "But I think that I already like him."

"That's okay, when I knew him, he was a likable fellow, funny too," R'gal recalled fondly.

"Yes, he does make me laugh." She smiled as she too remembered something.

"But your relationship can never progress beyond a friendship." He shared this truth with compassion.

"What do you mean?" She did care for him, perhaps already too much.

"You could never marry him and have children," he tried to state it simply.

"But why not?" It seemed beyond her capacity to understand.

"Because he is an angel, he was never intended to have offspring. The joining of the human and angelic races would be unnatural." He could think of no easier way to say it.

She stood, offended. "I think you should leave!"

R'gal also stood. "I'm sorry, there was no easy way to say that. Before I leave may I ask one final question?" He paused hopefully. She took a shuddering breath, but nodded her assent. "Do you pray?"

"Do I what?" Her offense began to return.

R'gal was praying himself, silently, "Do you pray?"

"What difference would it make," a little curiosity returned, "if I did?"

"I would urge you to pray, before you go tonight, for clarity and courage."

"Courage, what for?"

"It takes courage not to do what everyone else is doing, but standing against the tide can make all the difference in the world." He felt Rayeh's help clearly.

"And who would you say I should pray to?" She seemed sincere.

"To the King of the Heavens," he stated simply.

"The one Haniel rebelled against?" Then she paused. "Does he have a name?"

"He has many, but Chayeem will do for now." Just mentioning his name seemed to electrify the atmosphere.

Demonstrating a little clarity already she stated, "Thank you, that must have been difficult." A small smile wistfully graced her face, "Please excuse me. I need some time to think."

R'gal bowed slightly, "Thank you for your time and consideration. I will be praying for you both." The portal opened again and R'gal stepped back through it.

Chapter Nineteen
Lucifer's Banquet

Convinced that his plan proceeded well, Lucifer, in all of his finery, looked at his guests who had already arrived. Although most of them seemed dirty and repellent to him, he knew he must at least give the appearance of enjoying their company. He stood just inside the gate to his expansive, immaculately groomed gardens and personally welcomed each guest as they entered. He did enjoy the way they fawned over him with bows, curtsies, and much deference in their speech. One of the princes of men, he didn't catch the name, introduced his wife and then his daughter. Lucifer paid special attention to the daughter.

"My Lord, let me introduce my daughter, Shadai," whom he turned towards. "This is Lord Lucifer." She offered her hand. He took it, brought it back to his lips, and lightly kissed it. He was the master of putting on airs.

"My dear, welcome to my party." The words, so smooth and powerful, totally covered up the way his complete focus on her shunned her parents. He drank in her beauty, her fragrance, her entire being, as he pondered, "To which of my angels will I give this one?" He passed all three of them off to one of his servants as another trio stepped through his gate. It was difficult to keep up appearances with each new group, but he was the master of appearances. He turned back to his garden gate from handing off this last group to be shocked speechless, a rarity for him. Before him stood Haniel and the most exquisitely beautiful young woman he had ever seen, short of Adam's wife at the beginning of time. He had to have this one for himself.

"Haniel, you didn't come with your twenty-one." It was more a statement of fact than a question.

Haniel seemed taller than Lucifer, but it was just a trick of the light. "I sent all twenty-one of those you asked of me, sir," the 'sir' being spoken to Lucifer as an equal rather than as a subject.

Lucifer countered, a bit off stride, "Yes, yes, you sent all twenty-one, but why did you not count yourself in that number?"

Haniel looked to Judith, "I would think it obvious. Let me introduce Princess Judith." She did not offer her hand. Lucifer reached out his own to receive hers and she just looked at his hand. He withdrew it, a little shocked, but now wanting her even more. Her confident purity absolutely entranced him. She was just like Dawn at the beginning.

Lucifer smoothly covered his own embarrassment, "Yes, well, welcome to my party." He tried to catch Judith's eyes, but she looked elsewhere. "Well, I hope to see more of you, Princess Judith." At her name, Judith looked him straight in the eye, not with disdain, but not with deference either. She and Haniel were definitely well matched. She turned back to Haniel as she said, "Thank you for bringing me." She looked ahead towards the festivities, took his hand, and practically dragged him towards them. Haniel smiled while Lucifer nodded in deference towards Judith and Haniel as he walked away with her. Lucifer stood there even more shocked and surprised, until the next group walked through his gate calling out, "Lord Lucifer," in greeting.

While taller than most of the men, Lucifer no longer felt regal. He told himself that not sitting on his dais made him feel diminished. After the last of his guests arrived, he mingled among them, keeping mostly to those men of less stature and their women. In the middle of the garden stood five large tables replete with fresh fruit and prodigious amounts of wine. Most of the daughters of men had paired up with an angel, in their human form of course. The fallen angels had lost the ability to transfer to their angelic, winged versions of themselves after the rebellion. A majestic bell sounded and the conversation subsided. Lucifer stepped up onto the first of the stairs that led into his palace banquet hall and announced, "Join me for dinner." He held out his left hand to Shamair, the daughter of the proclaimed king of men, Amthael, who, while not as shockingly beautiful as Judith, was still striking in her own right.

Judith laced her arm through Haniel's. While not having had the opportunity to talk with him about R'gal's appearance, she did continue to ponder what R'gal had said in her heart. She had even made her first attempt at praying to Chayeem and although not sure what she was supposed to expect, had felt somewhat better afterwards. They headed towards the banquet hall as she whispered, "I have something important to talk to you about later." He hoped it was something wonderful, but could only tell from her tone that it was important. He reached over and squeezed the hand that held his arm.

The scrumptious banquet tables were filled with steaming, nearly raw meats, cooked and raw vegetables, rice, a variety of steaming broths, and a large assortment of fruits. Lucifer stepped up to the first table with king Amthael, who leaned over and whispered something in Lucifer's ear.

Lucifer nodded and the king announced, "To all my subjects and those who belong to Lord Lucifer, we are expecting an incredible evening. I can tell, just looking at the food, that our expectations are going to be exceeded. Please show your thanks to our host," and he began to applaud. The room nearly shook as the entire assembly raucously joined in.

Lucifer basked a moment in the chaos and then raised a hand for silence. When he finally received it, he added, "May this be the beginning of the complete integration of our two kingdoms, cultures, and families. You may now go serve yourselves." The applause broke out again. While the rest of the guests headed towards the banquet tables, Lucifer, Shamair, Amthael, and his wife headed to the head table. Raised on a platform a cubit higher than the rest of the floor, it dominated the room just as Lucifer had designed it. There were cushions around it for up to sixteen people. Lucifer, Shamair, Amthael, and his wife all reclined at the table. Servants rushed to fill their plates with food and their goblets with wine. Raziel, a lovely young woman, and what Lucifer assumed to be the young woman's parents arrived at the head table shortly after Lucifer and his companions.

Amthael leaned over and whispered, "Your commander has chosen well. That is Cozbi, the daughter of my first counselor." He looked around, "Where is your other commander?" Lucifer pointed off to the right, on the main floor, where Haniel and Judith sat with her parents. Amthael added, "He has also chosen well. Judith is the daughter of one of my most valiant princes."

Lucifer wondered why Haniel had chosen to sit on the main floor rather than at the head table with him and Raziel. Was it a strategic mistake, a stroke of tactical brilliance, or just a random chance? Knowing Haniel, he doubted that chance played a role in his decision at all. Humor, maybe, chance, no!

Servants also bustled among the tables on the floor, keeping all the guests' goblets continually filled. The eating and drinking continued for hours, and things were getting louder, more raucous by the moment, until Lucifer rose to announce, "I have prepared all the bedrooms on all the floors of the east wing for your pleasure. I would only ask that you enter discretely in case the room is already occupied." General laughter and elbow throwing followed as he continued, "also, the dance floor is open for those who need another form of exercise," and he pointed to the west where the sun set in a stunning display of colors. Many couples struggled to their feet, or depending on their level of intoxication staggered, some to the dance floor, others to the bedrooms.

Chapter Twenty
Heaven's Counsel

Back in heaven, the archangels reclined around the table, goblets in hand. Rayeh addressed them all with, "Well, how did you think it went?"

Uriel began, "Lucifer was offended. I expected no less. I suppose that I should have expected more. He argued for 'free will' and I reminded him that even Chayeem's patience has a limit. He declared that he would press all the way to that limit and I'm sure he will even go beyond."

Rayeh added, "I'm sure that none of us are surprised there, but we had to try. Thank you, Uriel." He looked around the table, "Gabriel?"

"My experience with Raziel was similar." He took a swallow from his goblet. "He was with twenty of his best soldiers and I thought I was going to have a fight on my hands, but when I drew Kol they all froze with their hands upon the hilts of their swords. I also threatened him with the wrath of Chayeem, but he told me to leave them alone, they would do as they pleased."

The sadness was growing as Rayeh asked Raphael, "And how did Haniel respond?"

Raphael smiled weakly, "I may offer a small ray of hope. Haniel was at least welcoming, but he felt it too late to really do anything. There seemed too much momentum already gathered to the purpose of cementing this unholy alliance between angels and men. I tried to dissuade him and felt we connected at least in part. He does not plan on participating in the joining, but still feels he has to make a token appearance at the event."

Rayeh smiled too, "That does give us some hope. Then there is our secret weapon," and he laughed. "Tell us of your experience with the Princess Judith."

R'gal took a deep pull from his goblet, a deeper breath of air, and began, "I believe that we really do have some grounds for hope. Princess Judith is really something, someone wonderful. I don't know that I have ever met anyone that wonderful since Adam's wife, Dawn. There is a commanding purity about her that is unique on earth right now, I think. She and Haniel are already friends and I feel that lent itself to our rapport since we were friends too. She did not realize that we were both angels. She had no idea what that even meant. So, I showed her."

Raphael interjected, "And just how did you do that?"

"I became my winged form right before her very eyes. She about fell off the bench she was sitting on. I quickly turned back, but she still had difficulty believing that Haniel had been one of us. I cautioned her not to go any further in her relationship with Haniel and it was obvious from her response that she had already considered becoming his wife and raising children with him. I pointed out that half human, half angelic children were never meant to be, at which point she asked me to leave. Before I did, I asked her one final question: Did she pray? I think that totally caught her off guard and she began to realize the gravity of the circumstances from our perspective. I again urged her to pray as I left and I believe she will at least think more clearly about things."

"Thank you, R'gal. You will be pleased to know that she did attempt to pray. She wasn't sure what to expect, but at least she tried. She is virtually our only hope." Rayeh paused, "Now I have another interesting assignment for all of you." They all looked up, "R'gal, please turn into a horse."

R'gal got up from the table and suddenly a beautiful black stallion stood before them.

Almost in chorus they exclaimed, "You're kidding."

"I would like you each to become a horse. Simply say 'horse' in the same manner that you usually say, 'wings.'"

Raphael had the most difficulty, but soon there were the four of them standing there: black, gray, chestnut, and bay horses. A portal opened.

"I want you to find somewhere to stand around Lucifer's palace and garden as an additional deterrent to this spectacle." The three of them stepped through. Rayeh suddenly had a bridle in his hand and spoke to the only horse left. "R'gal, if you don't mind, I'd like to go with you and do something similar, but to do so I will need to lead you around by the nose, for a bit," and he smiled at the pun.

R'gal snickered as a horse, "Fine by me," and lowered his head. When he was through, Rayeh changed into his young man form. It had been quite some time since they had seen him like that. He smiled in answer to R'gal's unasked question. "It will seem less intimidating." R'gal nodded and the two of them walked through another portal.

Chapter Twenty-One
Opportunity

Many couples were dancing around the room together on the dance floor. The music that Lucifer had put together was particularly otherworldly, both evocatively and sensually. Most of the couples responded to it quite openly. A large number of other couples had made their way to the bedrooms Lucifer had offered and, in some cases, when a couple found people already there, they just joined them and increased the debauchery.

On the other hand, Haniel and Judith had walked out onto the veranda. As the sun set, they were surrounded with intoxicating twilight fragrances. The two of them sat overlooking the gardens, holding hands as they looked out into the growing darkness. Neither of them had said anything for the last couple of minutes.

Judith finally broached the subject that had been on her heart. "Your old friend R'gal stopped by to visit me."

Haniel was taken completely by surprise, "How would he know about us?"

"He also knew about Lord Lucifer's plans for tonight," she added.

"He did?" His voice was now tinged with a little fear. "What did he say?"

"He said that you haven't been completely honest with me." She was going straight to the point. "He said that you are not currently in a very good place."

Haniel had turned as white as a sheet. He was almost afraid to ask, "Anything else?"

She took a deep breath. "Yes, he said that you were an angel."

"What?" Could this get any worse?

"And then he turned into an eight-cubit tall winged man in battle armor right before my eyes." She had never seen Haniel like this. Before, he was always confident, self-assured, yet caring. Now he seemed diminished.

He had dropped her hand, hung his head, and looked at the floor. "Well, in most cases he is correct. I am or was an angel, but I have always tried to be honest with you. I...I just haven't told you everything." He looked back into her eyes.

"You didn't think this was important?" She wasn't really sure exactly how she felt about all of this. She just knew how she felt about him and how his withholding information seemed to tarnish everything.

"Well, no! Not yet anyway. I guess if we were just friends, I didn't think it made any difference." He was having difficulty treading along this uncharted pathway.

Judith continued with a little less passion, "R'gal said that we could NEVER become anything more than friends, that if I allowed our relationship to develop into more, into a marriage, then the joining of the human race and the angelic race would produce something unnatural." She was still saddened by this, "Are there other things that I don't know about you that I should know before this relationship goes any further?"

"Did he tell you why I can no longer assume my angelic form?" He seemed ashamed and somewhat afraid of what else might come between them.

She reached over and took his hand. "Yes." He smiled weakly as she added, "But I want to hear it from you. Tell me about the rebellion in heaven,"

Just when he thought things had taken a turn for the better, they made a U-turn. "Wow, this may take a while."

She smiled a little, "I think the rest are spending the night. So, I think we have the time."

Haniel took his own deep breath, "Okay, before the beginning of time as you know it, the King of the Universe made a race of beings called the angels. There were seven archangels over all the angels and over the seven of us there was our prince, Lucifer." He told her everything and when he finished there were tears in both their eyes.

She removed a delicate embroidered hand cloth from the sleeve of her dress to dab her eyes. Fortunately, she did not extravagantly paint them as most all of the other daughters of men did. No, her beauty needed little external enhancement. "And since your banishment you are restricted to your human form?"

He had wiped his eyes with his sleeve, "So far, yes."

She probed even deeper, "And if we marry and have children? Will they be unnatural?"

He was conflicted, feeling both the emotions of anger and sadness. "We don't really know; it's never happened before." He took a shuddering breath and then ventured into the dark. "You had thoughts of marrying me?"

She dropped his hand and her head, looking up shyly through her lashes. "It had crossed my mind."

Suddenly, a horse whinnied. Haniel looked out over the garden, startled. The soldier instincts ignited. In the torchlight he spied a young boy walking away from a majestic black stallion. He stood, sensing something amiss, the reverie broken. "Excuse me a minute." He reached for his sword, but remembered that he had not worn it. It was supposed to be a party.

The stallion remained there as Haniel strode down the veranda steps and across garden to where it stood. The boy was gone. The horse spoke, "Haniel?"

Haniel wished he had something in his hand, "What are you doing here?"

R'gal shook his head trying to dispel Haniel's atmosphere of offense, "Trying to reinforce what little hope is left."

"You can appear as a horse? You were the last one of us to even be able to appear as an angel!" It was near a sneer.

"I am here for you, Haniel, I am not here against you." He said this with great compassion.

"You met secretly with my Judith?" Haniel spit it out.

"If you mean that I didn't come flying in wearing full battle regalia, then yes, I guess it was secret. So, she told you?" R'gal asked softly.

"You said if we ever had a child that it would be unnatural!" His anger and pain returned.

"Perhaps a poor choice of words, but our two races were never designed to be mixed together."

"He said that, the Tree said that?" The question seemed sincere.

"He did."

"And you think you can stop us?" It was a challenge.

"Gently persuade you? That is my hope."

"Or what!"

"There is no implied threat here, just hope."

Haniel began, "My old friend you have gone too far. My relationship with Judith is not for you to meddle in. So, I believe your hope is in vain. All you have done is proven to me that I love her. I didn't think even that was possible, let alone that we would be capable of producing children." He turned and strode back to the veranda. R'gal hung his head in what he hoped was not defeat.

Haniel marched right back to Judith, got on one knee and asked, "Will you marry me?"

Shocked, Judith could say nothing, then finally, "What was all that about?" She pointed towards the horse.

"It appears my old friend, the archangel, can also impersonate a horse."

"That was your friend, the angel?" Her eyes had widened.

"Yes."

"And after talking to him you want to marry me?"

"Most definitely!" And he held her eyes for a long moment.

"I think that I suddenly like your old friend very much." She knelt with him and kissed him longingly. When she finally came up for air, smiling, she said, "Yes!" and kissed him again.

Chapter Twenty-Two
Counsel Debrief

Dejectedly, they all reclined at the table.

R'gal had arrived last, but spoke first, "We got soooo close."

Sadness pervaded the atmosphere. "Yes, I had hoped...." Rayeh left the sentence unfinished.

After another pause, Uriel spoke slowly, "What's next, judgment?"

Rayeh smiled weakly. "Mercy wins out over judgment. We'll have to see how things play out, but it doesn't look good."

"And in the meantime?" Gabriel asked.

"I guess we would call it 'business as usual' until we know more."

The angels each got up and passed through their individual portals, all except R'gal who had received a hand motion from Rayeh to wait.

As soon as the last portal closed, R'gal apologized, "I feel like I let you down."

Rayeh shook his head, "Quite the contrary. It's because of you that we still have an avenue of potential dialogue open with Haniel and Judith."

"Will she conceive after they are married?" he asked hesitantly.

"Yes, she will. She will soon have a bouncing baby boy."

"And what will he be like, half human and half angel?" He still hesitated.

"Well, we are exploring new territory here, but all indications are that he will start out pretty normally and that most of the differences won't begin to be seen until he starts to grow and mature, which reminds me. I have a new assignment for you," Rayeh's smile deepened.

R'gal looked a little skeptical. "You're sure I'm ready for this?"

"Because you are willing to rely so heavily on me, most assuredly." His smile had deepened even more.

"Okay, let me have it!" R'gal offered sheepishly.

"Mankind has an interesting custom, many actually, but this one is special. When a child is born, they will sometimes ask another individual to act as that child's 'godparent.'" He still smiled, although his tone was more serious.

"What on earth does that mean?" R'gal wasn't sure where this was going.

"If anything were to happen to the parents, the godparent steps in to take the child and raise him. He even participates in the child's upbringing while his parents are alive. There is usually a special bond between the two."

"And how does this happen?" He was still uncertain.

"Well, it would seem appropriate for a semi-divine being to have another divine being as a godparent, don't you think?"

"Why wouldn't Haniel ask Raziel?"

"They aren't on very good terms with each other at the moment. Raziel is too far under Lucifer's control. Haniel still thinks and acts independent of the rebels. I think if you go back to visit them, they may very well ask you to perform that function."

"But Haniel is still immortal, isn't he?" R'gal's concern grew.

"Yes, he is. This, however has more important implications for our on-going contact with him and his family." Maybe there was more that Rayeh was not telling him.

"Well," and R'gal paused to ponder, "I would be touched by the gesture if they asked me."

"All right, it's settled then." Rayeh seemed excited.

R'gal hesitated again, "In what form am I going back to them? Surely not the horse?"

Rayeh pointed at him, "That one," and a portal opened next to them.

R'gal finally smiled, remembering, "Wish me favor."

Rayeh nodded, "I'll do more than wish it," and in his hand appeared one of the old wooden swords that the archangels had used to learn swordplay so many years ago. "A gift for his son."

That nearly brought tears to R'gal's eyes. "Thank you."

PART FOUR
The Fallens' Offspring

Chapter Twenty-Three
Haniel's Home

On the other side of the portal, he found himself next to a road that he assumed would take him to Haniel's. He had never been there before, but it seemed to match the road that Raphael had described when he spoke of his time trying to dissuade Haniel from attending the banquet at Lucifer's. Haniel's property was bordered by a four-cubit tall laurel hedge which he walked along until he came to an arbored opening. There was no guard, not even a gate. It sat open and appealing. He took a deep breath and entered along the stone walkway.

He had personally seen the opulence of Lucifer's palace and grounds, and had heard of Raziel's from Gabriel. These grounds were designed to neither impress, nor mystify, nor confuse you. They were designed to make you feel at home. Pleasantly surprised and suitably impressed, R'gal walked between the two manicured lawns which stretched four stadia on either side of the walkway. The walkway itself was lined with two-cubit high flowering rose bushes, whose color changed with each bush, yet it didn't seem garish, or distracting, but appealing. He found that he actually slowed his pace to enjoy the flowers, especially their fragrance. Again, he noticed a hint of difference with each bush, never competing with, but always enhancing the next. It was a wonder to experience. The tidiness of it all impressed you with the care that must be taken every day to make it appear just like this. It must be nearly six stadia to where he assumed the palace sat in the grove of trees that began there on either side of the walk. Looking ahead, he spied two gardeners just before the trees on their knees working with the rose bushes. There was a man on the left and a woman on the right. They were human, not angelic, and could have been twins except for the differences in gender and length of hair. Her hair was pulled back and under a cap, which even disguised that difference to a degree.

R'gal's boots sang only softly on the walkway because of his slow pace, yet they both heard him and turned, remaining on their knees. The man rocked back as he looked up, "May I help you, sir?"

"Yes, are your master and mistress in?"

"Yes, our mistress is in labor and our master awaits the birth," he shared openly.

"Perhaps I should come back another time then?" R'gal hesitated while he also listened closely to Rayeh.

"I don't recognize you, sir, but you are obviously of royal rank. I'm sure the master would welcome you as a diversion on this day, as wonderful as it eventually will be." The gardener was exceptionally wise also.

R'gal looked to the woman for a counter opinion, but she smiled and nodded, "Yes, please go in. There will be a guard at the door to the house. His name is Tidal, but he is not as fearful as his name portends, especially to one such as you."

"Thank you," and R'gal added, "Your roses are the best of their kind I have ever encountered." They both blushed, embarrassed by the praise.

R'gal walked through the trees and into a small open courtyard before the palace. It didn't feel like a palace though. It felt like a home, perhaps because it wasn't all marble and stone, but mostly constructed of natural woods. The frames of the windows were metal, but somehow burnished in such a way as to not draw attention to themselves and away from the feeling of the house, but rather enhance that feeling. As predicted there stood an impressive angel before the door in his human form. He did appear fearsome and formidable himself, probably because he contrasted so drastically with everything else about the place.

That all changed when R'gal spoke his name, "Tidal, I have come to see your master, Haniel, and Judith, his wife."

He smiled, recognizing the authority of royalty and that of another angel, "And you are?"

R'gal had drawn the wooden sword and presented it hilt first to Tidal before Tidal could blink, let alone get his hand on the hilt of his own weapon, "Tell him an old friend is here to see him. I understand his wife is in labor and he might enjoy the distraction of meeting with me."

Tidal responded with, "Yes, sir!" He took the offered wooden sword, turned on his heel and went inside. He returned shortly with Haniel.

Haniel held the wooden practice sword back out to R'gal, "What are you doing here now?" He was not angry, just surprised.

"The sword is a gift for your son." He spoke with both compassion and pride for Haniel and Judith.

"My son, how do you know it will be a son?"

"You forget the King whom I serve." Now R'gal was proud in his own right, "But I am told congratulations will soon be in order."

Haniel started to blush at his forgetfulness, "Excuse me, I am a bit distracted."

"And rightfully so," R'gal conceded, "this is a big event."

"That's not the word you used last time," but the day's event took the edge off of what could have been anger.

"Yes, I'm sorry that what I had to say last time was so hurtful. I had hoped it would be helpful…" He did not finish the sentence, but appeared sincerely sorry.

"Well, well…" Haniel was surprised again, "come in then, come in," and he ushered him past Tidal and into his home.

They entered a receiving room. It was beautiful in every way, exuding the same peace and serenity that shown everywhere else.

"Where did you come by this incredible home?" R'gal marveled aloud.

"We built it from scratch. After I proposed to Judith on the night of the Black Stallion," and he chuckled, "we both gave ourselves to its construction and then its decoration. You've met Judith, so you know how amazing she truly is. Then once she conceived, we doubled our efforts to make it welcoming for the young one, my son, if what you say is true."

At that moment the air was split by a baby's cry, "Well, you will soon see," and R'gal reclined at the table. Haniel joined him. R'gal seemed surprised, "Aren't you going to go see him?"

Haniel laughed, "At this moment, the midwives rule my home. They will come for me when they deem it appropriate." He reached for something to drink.

A few minutes later, one of the midwives approached the table, "You may come and see your son now."

As he stood, he inquired, "May I bring my friend?"

"Certainly, my Lord." She bowed and turned to lead the way as though Haniel didn't know where he was going.

Chapter Twenty-Four
Haniel and Judith's Son

Judith lay on her bed, exhausted yet joyfully glowing. At her breast their son nursed noisily. When she saw R'gal she smiled deeply, "What a pleasant surprise. You're not 'horsing around' today?" and she laughed lightly, "You know, I have you to thank for this child. Because of your conversation with my husband that night, he proposed immediately, and we were married shortly thereafter." Haniel actually reached over and hugged him in gratitude.

R'gal lowered his head, "It was not what I had hoped for, but…." And he left the sentence incomplete.

They looked at each other, nodded, and voiced in chorus, "Forgiven."

"Do you have a name for him?" R'gal inquired.

"Well, we didn't know he was a 'he' until just now, but we had both a girl's and a boy's name prepared," Haniel replied, looking at his wife. She nodded. "His name will be Elah, although not formally for another week. That is the custom here."

"Elah, a terebinth, a formidable tree. That will prove appropriate," R'gal shared gladly.

Haniel shook his head, "I never know if you are speaking with prescient knowledge or just positive intent."

R'gal smiled knowingly, "Words are just words until they are fulfilled."

Haniel looked at Judith, "He speaks in riddles sometimes too," and then he looked back at R'gal. "Could you give us a few minutes? I'll meet you back in the receiving room," and he looked at the midwife.

"Yes, my Lord," and she looked at R'gal. "Sir?"

R'gal followed her back to the receiving room where a servant stood by to see to his needs. He reclined at the table.

"Wine, sir?" She had the pitcher in hand.

"Yes, please." She filled a goblet and handed it to him. He downed most of it in a single pull and set it down on the table. She promptly refilled it. He was glad that angels were not prone to getting drunk. He chuckled to himself, *"A drunken flying angel. Now, that would be a sight."* The servant offered him a plate of fruit. He looked for the deep purple one and chuckled again, picked a soft pink one, and bit into it. Delicious! He addressed the servant, "Have you served Haniel long?"

She smiled bashfully, "I came along with the princess. I have served her for many years."

He looked around, "This place is a wonder. You make it feel like home."

"That is our intent, sir."

"Well, you are certainly creating the right atmosphere," he added as he rose from the table.

She blushed at the praise, "Thank you, sir."

"My name is R'gal," and he offered his hand, palm up.

She placed her hand in his upturned palm, "Jaroah."

He kissed the back of her hand lightly, "and you reflect her light as the moon does the sun." He paused to look deeply into her eyes, "A pleasure to meet you."

Haniel walked into the room and exclaimed light-heartedly, "Are you flirting with the help?" Jaroah blushed even more deeply as she let go of R'gal's hand. "Just kidding, Jaroah. I see you have met R'gal, but be careful, he can be quite winsome." And he laughed. She offered him a filled goblet which he gladly received. "That will be all for now, Jaroah." She bowed slightly and left.

He looked into R'gal's eyes and held them. "You and I have something to discuss," but his tone was light-hearted.

"Becoming godfather to your son?" R'gal offered.

Haniel just shook his head, "How do you know this stuff? Judith and I just talked about it." R'gal simply pointed upward. "Ah yes, sometimes I forget how wonderful that was."

"Well, you have your own little piece of wonderful right here," and R'gal spread his arms to indicate all that was around them, "and now you add to it a son."

"Yes," he paused, "and you are right, that is what I wish to speak to you about. Do you know what it entails?"

"In broad general terms, I think so," he offered.

"So, what do you think? Will he let you?" It was Haniel's turn to point up.

"Yes, he will. He was the one who told me you might ask."

"And you've thought about it?" Haniel wondered if he should be worried.

"I have, and I accept. My only question is how we will pull it off without tipping off your prince and the others that I am here." Now R'gal showed concern.

"Hmm, typical of me, I hadn't thought that far ahead." He began to ponder the "how."

R'gal smiled, "I'm sure he," and pointed upward again, "has it all figured out."

Haniel reached out his hand and there may have been a tear in his eye, "Thank you, I really appreciate this. There is no one I would trust his care to more than to you."

Now there was a tear in R'gal's eye too, as he reached out to grasp Haniel's forearm. "I'll go see what his next step is." A portal opened next to him and he stepped through.

Haniel said wistfully to himself, "I miss portals almost as much as I miss wings," and the tear in his eye finally coursed down his cheek.

Chapter Twenty-Five
Godfather Planning

R'gal lounged at the table. While the fruit and drink were as excellent as always, his mind churned with the possibilities and problems in a future as Elah's godfather and guardian. He knew that he should leave it all in Rayeh and the Tree's hands, yet he still fretted. Perhaps it was because he found that he cared so much for Haniel, Judith, and their child.

A portal opened and Rayeh stepped up to the table. "May I?"

"Like you need ask?" R'gal chuckled.

"Just being polite," Rayeh added his chuckle, "it never hurts. Well, that turned out as we had hoped."

"Yes, but I'm worried how we will accomplish it without alerting Lucifer or anyone else." His worried look had returned.

"I have been examining a number of possibilities and I think I have come up with a good one," Rayeh still smiled.

"Should I be afraid to ask?" He wondered if he worried less or more.

"Have I ever asked a task of you that was beyond your capability to perform?" Rayeh almost laughed.

"Only to keep me humble and listening." Rayeh's infectious smile was getting the better of R'gal. "Am I going back again as a horse?"

"Nope."

Unfortunately, R'gal was not relieved with the answer. "What then?" and he almost cringed.

"A dog," and Rayeh's smile broadened again.

"You're kidding?" His concern was returning.

"Try it."

Well, if Rayeh said it was possible, it must be possible. "Did you have any particular breed in mind?" R'gal was shaking his head side to side.

"Basenji." Rayeh seemed to have pondered all the details.

"The small ones, with the curly tails, that don't bark, but sort of scream?"

Rayeh nodded "Yes, you know your breeds."

"Probably because you just put his picture in my mind," he said nonchalantly.

"Did I do that?" He pretended surprise.

"I'm pretty sure you did." Rayeh was having too much fun with this. R'gal didn't even wait for instructions, he just turned into a Basenji, male of course. "Do animals still talk? Do I?"

Rayeh seemed almost stunned at how easily R'gal had accomplished his transformation. "Wow! Good job. Have you been practicing on the side?"

"No, I haven't," said the dog, answering the second question.

"No, animals do not talk, so you will need to be especially careful who you talk to and whom you talk in front of." Rayeh did seem to be enjoying this.

"And you're pretty sure this will work." R'gal made it a statement not a question.

"Wanna go on a trial run?" A portal opened next to R'gal the dog.

R'gal looked at the portal, "Near Haniel's home I hope."

"You'll need a little time to get used to four legs again."

"Better than a monkey, I suppose."

"Yup, I tried that one and it didn't work near as well. Good favor."

The dog wagged his head, then his tail, and walked through the portal.

R'gal re-adapted to four-footed travel as quickly as he had changed into a dog in the first place. He walked through a forest, but could smell Haniel's roses in the distance. He ran along a trail, cavorted a little, even chased a squirrel up a tree. Then the tree line ended at the road he supposed would pass Haniel's. A chariot was moving down the road, driven by Haniel at a cantor. When it passed, R'gal ran out behind it, caught up to it, and leapt up onto the chariot's platform.

Haniel felt the dog's landing, turned, and was going to swat him back out of the chariot, when he heard, "Haniel, it's me."

Startled, Haniel almost fell out of the chariot himself, but catching his balance replied, "R'gal! Now you're a dog? Isn't that a bit beneath you?" He laughed at the pun.

"It was his idea," and he pointed his nose upward.

Haniel stopped the chariot. "Actually, it's probably a great idea. Who will even question my coming home with a dog as a present for my son?" He laughed again at the thought of it.

"You probably shouldn't address me by name and I will only talk back when we are alone." R'gal was being serious.

"Reggie," he grinned. "And I think the name suits you. This sounds like a plan. Are you an indoor or outdoor dog?"

"How should I know; I've only been a dog for a half an hour! I haven't even peed on a tree yet."

Haniel was grinning from ear to ear, "This is going to be hilarious. Instantly obedient, already house broken, what more could I ask for?"

R'gal continued, "Even tempered, loving, a great listener, brave, courageous, I could go on and on..." There was a hint of laughter in his voice too.

They left the horse and chariot at the stables and walked into the back of the house. Haniel removed his boots, hung his coat and sword, each on a peg, while Reggie sat just inside of the door. "You want to stay here by the door or do you want to follow me in?"

Reggie whispered, "How big of a surprise do you want this to be?"

"Right, stay there. I'll be back shortly," Haniel decided.

"You wouldn't have a bowl you could fill full of water for me?"

"Ah, good idea. Do you remember Jaroah? I'll send her back with it in a minute. I'll go find Judith and Elah," and he left him there at the back door, panting.

Jaroah returned with the bowl of water quickly. "Reggie?" Haniel had told her his name. Reggie wagged his tail furiously. She knelt, set the water down, and reached out a hand, palm extended. He sniffed her hand, tail wagging, then licked it. She scratched him behind the ear. He could get used to this. "What a nice boy," and she stood back up. He got up, went to the bowl, and practiced lapping. It wasn't as difficult as he thought it might be. He was still panting a little. He sat, then laid next to the bowl. She knelt down again, beginning to pet and scratch him. He wished he could purr.

Haniel and Judith walked through the doorway. Haniel led Elah by the hand since his eyes were closed. Judith reached up, pulled Haniel close, kissed him on the neck, smiling broadly. She obviously was okay with Elah having a dog.

Judith whispered, "Okay, Elah, you can open your eyes."

He was tall for a three-year-old, almost athletic on his feet. He opened his eyes and was speechless for a moment, then squealed, "A dog, you got me a dog!"

Haniel spoke authoritatively, "Yes, son, and you will have to learn to take care of him. His name is Reggie."

"Reggie," and he let the name roll off his tongue, "I like it, I like him. Can I pet him?"

Reggie stood, wagging his tail. Haniel instructed, "Lesson one, you approach a dog slowly, with your hand out, palm up, and see how he reacts." He demonstrated as he spoke. Reggie sniffed Haniel's hand, then licked it. Haniel stepped back.

Elam held out his hand and walked slowly forward, "Good boy, Reggie, good boy." Reggie sniffed his hand also and then licked it.

"Now, slowly kneel beside him, your hand still out," and he did, "then talk to him as you reach back and lightly pet him."

Elah followed those instructions to the letter also. When he did, Reggie stepped into him, still wagging his tail, and leaned against him. Elah put his arm around him and hugged him, putting his head down onto Reggie's. "I think he likes me."

"I'm pretty sure he does," and Haniel kissed Judith on the top of the head. Reggie and Elah each had a new friend.

Chapter Twenty-Six
Further Depravity

One of the fallen angels, Hathath, decided that laying with the daughters of men did not entice him at all. He lived out in the wilderness and the daughters of men were far too refined for his tastes. He liked his meat nearly raw. He needed something much more challenging, so he chose lying with a beast. It is still unknown how he was able to catch, seduce or sedate a lioness. Perhaps he just overpowered her in the wild, but the product of that union, carried to term, survived. The lioness did not. She died giving birth to the abomination that would be known as the Ariel. Initially, to Hathath it looked like a normal lion cub. Then the Ariel's front paws developed into hands and its whole upper body began to resemble the divine man that had produced it, except for its lion-like head. He trapped another lioness for her milk, but once weaned off of lioness' milk the Ariel began crawling on hands and paws, then quickly progressed to standing on its hind legs like a man and walking.

Hathath kept his progeny, Labee, secret, not an especially difficult task while hiding in the wilderness. If Labee did speak, only Hathath understood him and because they kept to themselves, no one else would either. That was fine with Labee. He didn't need to be understood, he needed to be feared. Hathath decided that he liked children so he lay with the lioness that had provided Labee's milk. She delivered a litter of two and she and both cubs survived.

At the age of six, Hathath began to teach Labee hand to hand combat. In the woods Labee ran down a deer, killed it bare-handed, ripped out its heart, and ate it on the spot where it had fallen. When Labee reached the age of ten, he stood nearly four cubits tall and Hathath introduced him to wooden swords. Hathath carved them from an oak he had felled himself and polished them to shine like metal. Labee proved equally skilled with both the right hand and the left. Fortunately, Hathath had carved enough swords for the entire family.

The day came when Hathath needed two real swords forged for Labee. There was rumor of a master swordsmith hidden deep in the forest. It was then Hathath discovered that, not only could Labee speak with him, but Labee conversed with most of the other animals. With their combined aid, all of them were able to find and track the smith, Robsar, back to his smithy at the fork of the river Peleg. The moment Robsar laid eyes on Labee, he was begging for the privilege of making his swords. It was rumored, but unsubstantiated, that Robsar had learned his skill from Alathos himself. Regardless, Robsar would soon become a legend for the swords he made for the Ariel. They were made of steel, forged from falling stars. With the two he made for Labee, Robsar would make him nearly invincible.

Labee's two half-brothers, Labah and Laesh, grew to become the warriors on his right hand and his left. Labah would fight on his right with only a sword in his right hand, and Laesh would fight on his left with a single blade in his left hand. The swords Robsar made for them were inferior, but adequate. No one had ever seen the three fight together. If they did, it would seem a sight spawned by the gods, because they were.

Although unknown to each other, Elah's training nearly mirrored that of the Ariels. By the time he was ten, he was taller, broader, and faster than his father. When they sparred with wooden swords, Elah bested Haniel seven times out of ten. Soon it would be every time. Elah had become a warrior, excelling in all forms of combat, with all manner of weapons, but he needed a new challenge. So, Elah became a scholar. With access to his grandfather's library, itself a legend in the area, he learned all the languages of man, both current and ancient. He devoured scrolls overnight and memorized everything that passed before his eyes. It was more to him than just information; he would figure out ways to incorporate it all into his life. He became a wise young man. His circle of friends was limited. With the growing depravity of men and angels, Haniel and Judith were very careful to watch over his selections. And he had Reggie. Elah found that Reggie seemed able to smell the bad friends and he wouldn't let Elah have anything to do with them, or at least would point them out and let Elah decided not to associate with them. The other offspring of the angels tried to recruit him, but he remained aloof, friends with only a select few of the children of men.

One afternoon, Haniel asked Elah to walk Reggie and they went off to play.

"I think it's about time we explain Elah's origin to him. What do you think?" Haniel desperately wanted Judith's opinion.

Judith's judgment was always sound. "We could give the help the night off and have Reggie there too to help with the explanation."

"After supper dishes?" Haniel suggested.

"That would be a good time for us and the servants."

Judith talked to the inside help and Haniel the outside help. All the servants were overjoyed to have a night off. They weren't even surprised or suspicious, as Haniel and Judith were appreciated and loved by their staff because they were used to being treated so well. They worked hard out of love not duty.

The dishes had been cleared and washed, and the staff had excused themselves. The family was still reclining around the table. Elah was deep in a scroll as usual with Reggie at his feet.

"Elah," he looked up from the scroll as Haniel continued, "How much do you know about your origin?"

"Is this the talk about the 'birds and the bees'?" Elah chuckled.

"No, son. Not that origin." Elah took after his dad, a lot. He wasn't going to make this easy, regardless.

"What then?"

"There are two races of beings on the planet, besides the animals and birds." Haniel was moving into his story-telling mode. "There is mankind and the angels. Your mother is from the race of mankind and I am from the angels."

"What's an angel?" Elah interrupted him.

"How about if I show him?" Reggie spoke for the first time in Elah's presence.

Elah looked at him, shocked beyond words, but finally managed to say, "Reggie...talks?"

They hadn't discussed this, but Haniel knew that R'gal's instincts were usually impeccable. He took a deep breath, but Elah interrupted again, "You've been with me all this time and thought it not important enough to let me know you could talk?" Reggie stood up and wagged his tail. "Don't you wag your tail at me!" He seemed a little hurt.

"It was mostly for your protection," Reggie began. "You see, I am an angel too, sent here for your protection. We had agreed that to keep you safe and my identity hidden, I should only speak to your mom and dad."

"So, everything I have confided in you, you went straight to my parents and told them?" Elah was wrestling with this whole thing.

"Never!" Reggie was firm. "I would never betray a confidence that you shared with me," he hesitated, "unless it were life threatening."

Elah was regulating his breathing as he had been taught. He seemed to have regained full control. "Okay, what were you going to show me?"

Reggie looked at Haniel for approval. He nodded his head. Without a sound an eight-cubit tall angel, with wings and all, dressed in full battle armor, stood where there used to be a dog.

Elah nearly fell over. "Dad, you can do that too?"

"I used to be able to, but not anymore, son," he said sadly. Reggie returned to his dog form.

"Anything else that I need to know?" He was almost afraid to ask.

"Only that all three of us love you more than words, or our lack of them, can ever say." There were tears in Haniel's and Judith's eyes. It is hard to tell when a dog is crying.

"Your parents and I haven't talked about this, but I know that you now best your dad almost every time with the sword. If we can find a place where you and I can spar secretly, I think I can take you to the next level," and he looked to Elah's parents for confirmation. He got it.

"I would have to spar with that?" and Elah pointed to where R'gal, the angel, had stood.

Reggie wagged his tail faster, "As a man initially, but maybe eventually as an angel. One more thing," and he looked at the parents again. "I would like their permission to tell you of what there is beyond this world. Perhaps they could take on a tutor and give this old dog form a rest."

Haniel looked at Judith. She nodded and said, "Yes, we would like that. My father's library can only teach him so much."

"Then it's agreed, if it's okay with you, son?"

"Yes!" he replied enthusiastically.

"I may need to be gone for a bit, to practice turning into a different man other than the one I usually become. I have never tried that before. When I return, I will be Ratah the tutor. I will also be a master swordsman, but we will keep that secret from all but the four of us."

"Not a problem. It won't take you that long. Time there doesn't flow like it does here," Haniel said, remembering.

Chapter Twenty-Seven
Coming of Age

Of the forty-two children that were conceived the night that the fallen ones lay with the daughters of men, ten did not come to full term. Another ten died during their birth and two more died as a result of early childhood accidents. That left twenty, plus Elah, to grow and mature into semi-divine beings. It was interesting that all of the offspring of the joining of the two races were male. What would later be discovered also was that they were all sterile. The fallen angel fathers of the twenty banded together to establish the Ashereem, a special school for their sons' training and development, headed by Lucifer himself, with Raziel as the headmaster. The Ashereem first formally convened when the boys turned six. Mornings, Raziel led them into the mysteries of what it meant to be divine, sharing a rewritten history from the beginning of all things until their current place in the world. As they grew and matured, he and their fathers taught them the principles of leadership. That they were a cross-breed was not seen as a stigma, rather a qualification to lead in the affairs of angels and men. They were, after all, the offspring of the angel commanders and princesses of men. Elah's upbringing was kept separate from the others by Haniel's proactive design. He did not want his son to become one of them.

In the afternoons they were taught hand-to-hand combat, wrestling, and a variety of martial art techniques. They learned how to use their opponents' force to their advantage. They learned strategy and tactics. At age ten, they were all nearly four cubits in height, and they began to learn the way of the sword. Each father presented his son with a wooden sword that the father himself had carved from the sacred oak. It was dried and hardened in their sacred fire, and was a formidable weapon even while only wooden. The Ashereem changed sparring partners each day in order to continue to excel and were all considered equal to one another, with the exception of Raziel's son, Mekaroth. He routinely bested them all, each and every day. "Whose turn is it to get beaten up by Mekaroth today?" became their daily mantra.

At the beginning of their twelfth year, Lucifer appeared, usually once or twice a week, to teach them tradecraft and intrigue. They all became exceptionally adept, but again, Mekaroth excelled beyond them all. As it approached the time for the lunar eclipse of their twelfth year, it was decided to hold a contest. It would be a single elimination tournament among the Ashereem. Lucifer secretly met with the legendary hermit smithy, Robsar, at his forge in the wilderness, and commissioned him to fabricate a sword of wonder. Robsar forged it out of the iron ore from another fallen star. Its only peer would be the swords of the Ariel Labee, and no one knew of his or his brothers' existence, not even Lucifer.

The story the four of them had concocted for the departure of Reggie involved him visiting a relative's farm. R'gal had provided a dog that looked just like Reggie to go out there and play the part. The ruse worked perfectly and included Haniel's introducing Ratah to the household staff as Elah's new tutor. Haniel also prepared a nearby meadow to become the new sparring area. It lay on the outskirts of his property, bounded by a thick growth of trees, whose entrance he protected with an iron-shod gate, with no way in or out of the area except by the gate. The dense forest secluded the field and Ratah had enlisted a number of birds to act as sentries during his training sessions with Elah, just in case anyone showed up unannounced. They trained there, in their secret forest pavilion, every afternoon. Haniel had lent his son his sword, "Hane," and Ratah fought with his own sword, "Shenah." The song of the two of them in concert would alone have brought people from miles around, if it were not for the sound-deadening quality of that ancient forest. Sometimes, their music was so wonderfully mesmerizing that the avian sentries had to be reminded that they were on duty.

In the mornings Ratah taught Elah sacred history, from the creation of the angels, the forging of the singing swords, through the fall of angels and the fall of mankind's original parents.

"So then, my father is one of the fallen angels?" It surprised Ratah that Elah hadn't asked sooner.

"Yes, he followed Lucifer in the rebellion and was cast from heaven to earth." It saddened him to have to explain it.

"Is there no way for him to redeem himself and rejoin you in heaven?" Elah pleaded.

"Hmmm, you've raised an interesting question. I'll have to get back to you on that, but for now, we have work to do." Ratah thought he had deflected that question rather well, but promised himself that he'd ask Rayeh later.

Ratah had perfected appearing as a shorter, nondescript human. He sometimes seemed so invisible to others that they walked right into him, "Excuse me, I didn't see you there," or "Hey, watch where you're going." During their second year of sparring, they went back to wooden swords for a while. Ratah taught Elah to fight equally well with both his right and left hand. Then, on what he thought was a whim, he taught him to fight with two swords. He had Haniel carve and fire harden two more swords. Haniel was overjoyed to do it. He would often steal away to their forest hideaway and watch the two of them sparring. He was exceptionally proud of his son.

Then came news of the "Coming of Age" contest. Set for the time of the lunar eclipse, it had nearly everyone coming to the special grounds that Lucifer had created for the event. There would be feasting, music, dancing, and the festivities would conclude with the contest. It was rumored that the winner would be crowned a prince, be given a princess and a gift of wonder from Lord Lucifer himself. Haniel and his family would attend, but Elah had no intention of competing. None of Lucifer's gifts enticed him in the least.

Chapter Twenty-Eight
An Ariel in the Contest

Hathath had heard the rumors about the "Coming of Age" contest for the semi-divine boys when he went into town for supplies. This made him decide to have his own coming of age ceremony for his son Labee. Hathath snuck silently into the city one night, knocked a young virgin girl unconscious, kidnapped her, and presented her to Labee. The Ariel didn't know what to do with her. Should he eat her? After toying with her for a while, she woke up, and started screaming. He took her, struggling in his arms, back to Hathath and said, "Thank you for the gift, but I don't want her. You can return her to wherever you found her." Hathath knocked her unconscious again, took her back near her home, and left her. No one would ever believe her story that a half-lion, half-man, lived in the forest, anyway.

Then the thought crossed his mind, "What if I enter Labee in the contest?" He began planning how he could accomplish it. He fabricated a long, hooded robe that completely covered Labee and his two swords. They would sneak in at the end of the contest, at the height of the eclipse when the only light came from torches. All eyes would be focused on the final contestants, and whoever won, Labee could challenge to final combat, to the death. By the day of the contest, Hathath and his son were fully prepared.

Lucifer's contest field was controlled chaos, just the way he liked it. It seemed the entire town had shown up. Why wouldn't they? There was everything here a man could desire: food, drink, music, dancing, carousing, fighting, and all the passions unbridled. At the height of the frenzy and the beginning of the eclipse, the contest began. The twenty Ashereem paired up, by lot, for their first match; all ten matches were conducted simultaneously. The ten winners drew lots to pair up again. Raziel's son, Mekaroth, won his next match easily. He was done long before all the others completed theirs. Lots were drawn between the five winners and Mekaroth did not have to fight in this round. Two more were eliminated and lots were drawn between the three remaining. This time Mekaroth fought and again easily defeated his opponent, practically beating him senseless. After taking a small respite and drinking copious wine, Mekaroth was ready for the final match. They sparred for a bit until his opponent took a misstep, overcommitted a thrust, and Mekaroth knocked him unconscious with the hilt of his sword. There was thunderous applause, yelling and screaming, as Raziel stepped up to embrace his son.

A loud roar stilled the raucous celebration. Words split the air, "He has not won!" and there stood Labee unrobed, his father Hathath behind him. He roared again, removed one of his swords and gave it to his father, "But this will be a fight to the death!"

Suddenly Lucifer stood in the center of the field, "Raziel, do you agree to this?"

Raziel could not lose face in front of the people and angels. "Mekaroth has fought three times already."

Hathath laughed, "Making excuses? Ask the lad." Raziel turned to his son.

"I'm fine, father. Let me kill this animal," Mekaroth sneered confidently. Raziel nodded and stepped away. Lucifer drew his own singing sword and handed it to Mekaroth, who bowed to receive it.

If this had been the last battle of the night, it surely would have become the stuff of legend. The ferocity of Labee's attack had the crowd speechless. He drove Mekaroth all over the field. Mekaroth's defense was impeccable, but not nearly enough to spare him. He finally faulted and Labee knocked him to the ground. Before he could deliver the mortal blow another voice split the air.

"No!" Elah stood there with his father's sword Hane in his hand.

Labee roared and Hathath interpreted, "You would defy my son his kill?"

"I would," and with the swinging, singing sword swirling about him, Elah advanced toward the Ariel.

"Then my son will slay you, instead!" shouted Hathath. Lucifer appeared next to Labee from somewhere, took the sword from the fallen Mekaroth, and traded Labee for the sword in his hand. Lucifer proclaimed, his face a mask of maniacal glee, "To the death!"

The clash of the two singing swords was cataclysmic. Lucifer's sword, Dawn, created flashes of lighting and thunder in concert to Hane's symphony as the eclipse became total. The cuts, parries, thrusts, blocks, turnings, and deflections were occurring faster than the eye could record. They went on and on beyond what any human could possibly endure. But then, these were not humans. They were both semi-divine beings and this battle proved it. Finally, Elah parried a blow, countered, and disarmed the Ariel. Unarmed, Labee roared, crouched, and lunged at Elah who slew him in the midst of his attack. The Ariel's body disappeared from this plain of existence.

Hathath's cry split the sky, "By the blood of my son, I will have my vengeance for his death."

Haniel stepped into the torchlight, "You have no grounds for that oath. You agreed to this death match."

Elah reached down, picked up Lucifer's sword, and threw it to him where he stood.

Lucifer cackled, "By right of conquest, you have won the two swords of the Ariel."

"I have no need of them," Elah announced as he turned to leave.

"And the prizes for winning this contest?" Lucifer dangled behind him.

"I will take the sword of Robsar, that is all. You may keep your title and princess." He had to tread carefully. To make Lucifer an enemy would be foolish, but wisdom called Elah to stand up before him. He walked to Lucifer and reached out for the sword. He did not kneel or bow. Lucifer was tempted to cut off the extended hand, but instead handed him Robsar's sword, to the thunderous applause of the people.

Lucifer thought to himself, *"I will have to watch that one also."*

Hathath melted into the crowd and disappeared.

Elah walked to his father, then to his mother and his tutor, and together they turned towards home. The crowd continued to applaud their departure.

Elah turned to Ratah and whispered, "Couldn't you turn into three horses? It's a long way home."

They all chuckled.

Chapter Twenty-Nine
After the Contest

It took nearly a week for things to return to normal. There were so many well-wishers showing up daily to congratulate Elah on his victory that Ratah was relegated back to the form of Reggie the dog who had returned from the farm. They were able to sneak away a few afternoons for some practice at their forest training field where Reggie turned back into Ratah and allowed Elah to get used to his new sword. While not a singing sword, Robsar had forged a sword of wonder. Elah continued to grow into his manhood and excel in his swordsmanship. They were all very proud of him.

One afternoon as they practiced, there was a frantic knocking at the iron clad gate. Ratah quickly turned back into Reggie the dog. Who, they wondered, had discovered their secret place? It turned out to be only one of the servants. Haniel must have given him directions.

"Lord Lucifer is at the house. He seeks an audience with you, young master." The servant was literally shaking in his boots. This was odd, Lucifer usually commanded you to an audience at his palace. He rarely ever would come to someone's residence and ask for an audience.

Elah smiled, "Return and tell him I will be there shortly," and then wondered how long he should let him wait.

Reggie answered the thought of his heart after the servant was out of earshot with, "Don't let Lucifer wait too long or he will come searching for you."

Elah sheathed his sword. He and Reggie left the field, locking the gate behind them. It would appear that the two of them had just been out for a walk.

Haniel entertained Lucifer in the receiving room as Elah and Reggie arrived. They entered through the back, where Elah hung up his cloak and his sword, and splashed some water in his face. Reggie and Elah entered the receiving room where Haniel and Lucifer lounged at the table.

"Lord Lucifer," he bowed slightly, "you wished to see me?"

Lucifer was a master at doling out praise while remaining condescending, "Come, join us. Raziel will forever be in your debt for saving his son and destroying that awful beast."

Elah nodded, "And what happened to it? I slew it and it disappeared?"

The question befuddled Lucifer for a moment, "Ah…there are a number of theories, but we have no evidence to support any of them. They are all simply conjecture," and he seemed to have gotten himself out of that conundrum.

"So, what can I do for you?" Elah asked, trying not to be condescending himself. He must not press Lucifer too far.

"I think it would be more appropriate for me to ask you, what can I do for you?'" He certainly appeared sincere, but Elah knew better.

"I have Robsar's sword. It is enough," he answered the question.

"Yes, it is a wonder, but I desire to do more." Lucifer sounded like he was fishing for something.

"As I said, the sword is enough," which sounded to Lucifer like, "Didn't you hear me the first time?" Lucifer chose to ignore the tone.

"But…" and he hesitated, "with my extensive connections throughout the known world, I could find you a match suitable to your position."

"Thank you, but I'm not interested." He was almost dismissive to Lord Lucifer. "Is there anything else?" Reggie began to growl from a menacing crouch.

"What's the matter with your dog?" Lucifer inquired with disdain.

"I don't think he likes you," and a faint smile graced Elah's face.

"Humph! No, that is all," Lucifer tried to dismiss Elah.

"I'm off to my studies. Father, we can talk later." Elah turned to go and Reggie let out a trademark Basenji scream and rose to leave with him, while Lucifer shrank back in fear.

Finally calming back down, Lucifer sputtered, "Where did you find that most disagreeable beast?"

Haniel smiled fully, "I came across him in my travels. He and Elah are practically inseparable."

"Humph," Lucifer struggled to his feet, obviously put off his game by this entire exchange. It had not gone at all as he had planned, nor as he had thought that he had foreseen. He almost had difficulty walking.

Haniel took his arm and escorted Lucifer to the door and into the care of his guards, where he seemed to regain something of his composure.

That night at supper, as they lounged around the table, Elah brought it up. "So, Lucifer wants to set me up with some princess. Is this his attempt to gain some measure of control over me?"

"It's difficult to say with Lucifer. Wheels within wheels, within other wheels. Things are never straightforward with him." Haniel spoke plainly. They trusted all the staff implicitly and were accustomed to speaking their mind even with them in the room. The staff were considered and treated as family.

"While we are on the topic of setting Elah up with someone, I have some suggestions," Judith looked coyly at Haniel.

"I'll bet you do," his eyebrows raised, "and who is it, if I may ask?"

"You may. It's Japhia, my sister's daughter." Her coy smile broadened.

"Ah, that one," Haniel looked to Elah. "Do you know her?"

"I do, and she reminds me much of you, Mother." A smile began to grace Elah's face. "May I ask her father if I can court her?"

"That would be a welcome change from what the other Ashereem would probably do." Haniel looked at Judith, who nodded her approval. "Would you like me to talk to her father, or your mother talk to her mother?"

"Ratah, would you like to weigh in on this conversation?" He was at the table as Elah's tutor tonight and not just as his dog.

Ratah appreciated being included. "I would weigh in on the affirmative, but I have a question."

"Sure, anything." It was nearly a chorus.

"Does she like dogs?" and he chuckled deeply.

Chapter Thirty
Questions

Well, lots of interesting events have transpired. How are you feeling about them?" Rayeh seemed truly interested.

"I have lots of questions," R'gal began with concern.

"That's why we are here. Can I pour you a drink?" There seemed a definite lilt of hope in Rayeh's voice as they lounged at the table.

"Yes, please. First question, can Haniel be restored to heaven?" He almost blurted it out.

"Wow, let's start with the easy one." He shook his head side to side negating his own statement. "Let me begin with an axiom, a truth, 'Mercy triumphs over judgment.' That does not say that there is no judgment. Without judgment there is no consequence to breaking the natural and moral law. However, as a foundational principle, there is always mercy available. Next, does my knowledge of a future event predestine it to happen. Not if I keep it to myself. But what if I tell you what is going to happen? Then it might seem there is only the appearance of free will and not the actual fact that free will exists. Finally, after having participated in heaven, if you choose to leave it, will you ever truly want to return?" He paused, "My question to you is, 'Are there any others of the 'fallen' besides Haniel who have expressed any interest in returning?'"

"I don't know of any others besides Haniel that might desire to return, and the question originates from his son, Elah." That was the quick and easy response. "What if he is or was the only one desiring to return? Would you let him?"

"And the question just before that, about truly wanting to return?" Rayeh kept him thinking.

"I guess I would say, a choice is just a choice, but some have monumental consequences." He pondered his answer. "I know he chose to follow Lucifer, but I'm not sure why. I know he chose to marry Judith, even after my inept attempt to dissuade them. However, the way he lives is different from all of the rest of the fallen, so is the way he has kept Elah apart from the rest of the Ashereem. Does all of that not count for something?"

"So, can he work his way back into our good graces? Is it possible for him to prove he is worthy of our trust once again?" More questions from Rayeh.

"Are you asking me to answer those questions or asking them on behalf of yourselves?" R'gal was getting confused.

"It is not my intent to confuse you, but to help you appreciate the gravity of what you are asking." Rayeh's voice and demeanor were calming to R'gal.

"I don't know, perhaps I have grown too fond of them all," he said sadly.

"R'gal, I don't think that is possible. You can never love too much, only inappropriately."

"Another axiom?" R'gal smiled a bit.

"Perhaps, but I have another question for you," he paused for effect. "Has Haniel ever prayed to me since he left heaven?"

"Not in my presence, but what about my absence?" he replied hopefully. "Can I broach that and the subject of his return with him?"

"How did your last attempt to persuade him go?" He was not finding fault.

"Yes, there is that," he sighed deeply.

"Now that I have answered those so succinctly, what other questions do you have?" It was hard to tell if he was serious or not.

R'gal hesitated, "Does Haniel's state preclude Elah's coming to you?"

"I did ask for this didn't I?" and he seemed to contemplate his answer. Maybe he was just stalling. "Each person is ultimately responsible as an individual. While action as a group may incur group consequences, the individual is still responsible for choosing to act with that group. So, the simple answer to your question is, no, but some group behavior overrules and predicates an individual's action."

Although he seemed to have gotten some answers, his heart was still unsettled.

"I know, R'gal, your heart is still unsettled, but that's as good as I can do at the moment." The compassion in Rayeh's voice was noticed by R'gal.

"Well, thank you for trying." R'gal truly did appreciate what Rayeh had said. It would take some time for him to process it all.

A portal opened, R'gal got up from the table and stepped through it, still contemplating what had been said.

He found himself, in his dog form, at the edge of the forest and the road that led to Haniel's home. He stepped out onto the road and trotted the short distance to Haniel's. The guard at the door reached down, "Reggie old boy, how are you?" as he scratched him behind the ear and let him into the house. He loped up the stairs and into Elah's room. Elah was still asleep. Reggie circled twice in front of the bed and then laid down to wait for him to awake.

Elah's eyes blinked open and he smiled. He had been dreaming about Japhia. They were becoming good friends. They had been walking through the forest, hand in hand, towards his training ground. That was interesting, because he hadn't held her hand yet. Well, now he knew that he wanted to. He wondered, *"When would it be appropriate?"* Then he noticed Reggie on the floor beside the bed. His smile broadened, he sat up, and tapped the bed beside him. Reggie got up, jumped up on the bed, lay down beside him and put his head in his lap.

"Reggie, I have just had the most wonderful dream. I dreamed that Japhia and I were walking hand in hand on the way to the training ground. Could it be a prophetic dream?" his words tumbled over each other in the throes of excitement.

"Was I with you?" Reggie mumbled in his lap.

"No, I don't think so. It was just the two of us." He was calming down a little.

"Then it was probably just a dream, otherwise I would have been with you too. You have never been to the training ground without me, have you?" his tail thumping on the bed.

"No," and he smiled mischievously, "but with her I might make an exception."

Reggie poked him in the ribs with his nose, "Not a good idea." He looked up in his eyes, "Should we get up and have some breakfast?"

That afternoon Elah and Japhia found themselves alone, walking towards the training ground. Elah looked around. Reggie was nowhere to be seen. He'd given him the slip. He reached over and took her hand. She smiled up into his eyes and leaned into him.

"Would you like to see where I train?" he lightly squeezed her hand.

"I would," and she squeezed back.

"It's just up ahead." He could see the iron clad gate. They walked up to it, he unlocked it, and opened it for her. She walked in and he followed.

Out of the forest crashed Labah and Laesh, the two Ariel brothers of Labee whom he had slain at the contest while saving Mekaroth. The two Ariel ran out in front of Elah and Japhia, ravenously growling and brandishing their swords. They spread out, preparing to attack from his flanks. Elah had stepped out in front of Japhia while drawing his own sword. The three swords of Robsar were about to clash when a portal materialized behind Japhia and R'gal ran through it. He called out Elah's name and threw his singing sword hilt-first toward him, as he pulled Japhia back through the portal and it closed. Elah caught R'gal's singing sword and with both swords swirling around him, attacked the brothers before they could attack him. R'gal's swinging, singing sword seemed to disorient the brothers for a moment, but they quickly refocused their attention and mounted their own attack.

R'gal's portal opened in Haniel's living room. He stepped out and bodily pushed Japhia towards the cushions shouting, "Elah is under attack at the training ground." He did not wait for Haniel to respond, but stepped back into the portal and it closed. It reopened back in the training ground. The ferocity of the Ariels' attack had put Elah totally on the defensive, parrying blows for his life. R'gal's stepping through the portal momentarily distracted him and while blocking Labah's blow, allowed Laesh's thrust to break through Elah's defenses. R'gal pulled him back through the portal mortally wounded.

"I suppose this is the end?" Elah whispered as R'gal laid him at the feet of Rayeh. R'gal looked hopefully at Rayeh, took his singing sword back from Elah and stepped back through the portal to find Haniel entering the training field at a run, his singing sword whirring around his head. Together they met the Ariel, who found themselves no match for two archangels wielding Hane and Shenah. They were dispatched quickly to the world of the dead.

The two stood there panting heavily. "And my son?" ventured Haniel.

"I left him at the feet of Rayeh," R'gal replied solemnly.

Haniel dropped his sword on the parched grass that marked the departure of the Ariel into oblivion, fell to his knees, emitted a cry of anguish that split the skies, and beat the ground until his hands were bloodied. When the sobbing ceased, a darkness crept slowly across Haniel's face. He weakly stood and then faced R'gal.

"He is dead, isn't he?"

R'gal hung his head, "I fear so." R'gal nearly sobbed himself.

"I will never forgive him for this. When I met Judith, I felt my heart begin to beat again. With the birth of my son and your return I also began to believe there was hope once more. How then could he take my son, after all I have tried to do?" He spoke haltingly.

"But we saved Japhia…" He never finished the sentence.

Haniel slowly stood. "If my son is gone, what use is his 'godfather'? Leave me! I never want to see you again!" The bitterness in those words stung R'gal to the core. Haniel strode dejectedly out of the training field. He didn't even retrieve his sword.

Chapter Thirty-One
Aftermath

Rayeh lounged at the table. A full goblet awaited R'gal.

"So, what happened to Elah?" he asked tentatively.

"I'm taking care of him, that should be enough," Rayeh responded firmly.

"And was that what you had foreseen?" His voice filled with sadness.

"Yes, I'm afraid it was." He said matter-of-factly, "Would it have done any good for you to have known beforehand too? If it would have, be assured that I would have told you. However, if I had, you would only feel more guilt that you were unable to fully intervene in the events to create a more desirable outcome. So, take heart, you are not at fault. If anywhere, the fault lies with me for having once again pushed Haniel into making another poor decision. That one pretty well cements things for him." He paused and took a long pull from his goblet, "Remember, you were able to bring Elah to me, you were able to rescue Japhia, and I assure you that the hearts of Judith and Japhia remain free from bitterness. There is grief, but no bitterness."

"And what of the Ariel?" It was a fair question.

"There will be more of them, a testimony to the growing depravity of men and angels." Sadness now shadowed his words too.

"And the Ashereem?" It was almost as if R'gal looked down the hallway into the future.

"The forty-two initial unions between the fallen and the daughters of men will replicate themselves throughout the ranks of the fallen which will breed further things unnatural." The sadness grew, "and the wickedness of man will continue to grow until it results in unthinkable evil." He took another long pull from his goblet, refilled it, and finished speaking, "the future is bleak indeed, but not without hope. There is always hope."

Japhia and Elah had been the same age when the Ariel slew him. His mother, Judith, had also fallen in love with Japhia during the short time that her son had courted her. Their shared grief for his loss brought them even closer together. Judith eventually asked her sister if Japhia could move in with them. Her sister had many other children and seemed almost glad to have one less.

She broached the topic with Haniel, "What would you think of Japhia coming to live with us?"

"Why would we want to do that?" He lived most of his life under a cloud nowadays.

"You know that I cannot have other children," the birth of Elah had rendered her barren. "She could become like our own daughter. She is a comfort and a joy."

He waved his hand at her dismissively, "If you'd like." And that was that. Haniel had moved out of their bedroom after Elah's loss.

Eventually, Haniel moved out of the house entirely. He built himself his own small house next to the training ground where he practiced feverishly every day after Elah's death, hoping it would ease the pain of his grief. He began to spend time in Lucifer's court, for which Lucifer was very pleased. Lucifer had feared he would lose Haniel, but when Haniel's son was killed he returned to Lucifer with an insatiable passion that only seemed satiated by sweat. Slowly, cautiously, craftily, Lucifer led him back into the inner circle and the darkness of his power. Haniel seemed to throw caution to the side.

It took years, but Judith and Japhia's love for each other provided fertile ground for the healing of their grief. One morning Judith recalled all those years ago when R'gal asked if she prayed. She remembered trying to pray without much success. She was about to start trying again when a portal opened and through it walked a dog.

"Reggie, is that you?" she asked tearfully.

"Yes, ma'am, it is," he replied, tail wagging. She knelt down and threw her arms around him, buried her face in his neck and wept softly. Into her tears he whispered softly, "Haniel said that he never wanted to see me again, but I don't remember you agreeing to that. So, I have been waiting for this day."

"I was about to try again to pray," she confessed.

"I know, he heard your heart before the words left your mouth," he whispered compassionately. "You were asking for help, especially with Japhia's future and that's why I am here. With your permission I would like to become her guardian and godfather."

"That would be wonderful." She pulled a kerchief out of her sleeve and wiped her eyes.

"I will need to change a little. Haniel would recognize me in this form. Would that be alright?" She nodded her approval and he changed into a Saluki. He was a light fawn color, half again the size of the Basenji, and a female.

She smiled, "That is perfect. We will need a cover story about where you came from that will convince Haniel." They put their heads together to come up with one. Rayeh had already given him some direction.

After supper, Japhia was in the kitchen helping with the dishes. She didn't need to be, but she liked to help, and the servants loved her even more for it.

Judith walked back into the dining area and broached the subject with Haniel, "I was coming home from shopping today and a dog followed me home. Can we keep it for Japhia?"

Haniel looked momentarily startled. "Let me see it!" Haniel's words were tinged with anger and apprehension.

She rose, left the room, and returned with a light fawn, female Saluki on a leash.

Haniel also stood. He took a menacing step towards the dog, his hand on the hilt of his sword, "You're not R'gal, are you?" His words held an obvious challenge.

The dog growled, baring her teeth. "Well, for starters…if you'll look, she's female. Could an angel appear as a female? Also, it's clear she doesn't like you and R'gal was your friend until you sent him away."

Haniel looked sternly at the dog, slowly removed his hand from his sword's hilt, and let his features soften. He knelt, held out a hand palm upward, and spoke softly, "Come here, girl. Come." It was less a command and more of a supplication. The dog seemed unconvinced, but her growling lessened and finally ceased. She walked forward hesitantly, sniffed his hand, looked him in the eye, then put her head back down, and licked his hand. "Have you showed the dog to Japhia yet?"

"Not before clearing things with you," she said demurely.

Haniel acquiesced, "Alright, if Japhia likes her, then she can stay,"

Judith stepped next to Haniel's kneeling form and hugged his shoulders to her leg, "Thank you."

Haniel left the house and returned to his own.

Chapter Thirty-Two
Judith's Dog

In the main house a cozy fire had been laid in the fireplace. Judith reclined in a chair in front of it, the dog sleeping at her feet, not visible from the doorway. Japhia walked in.

"I have a surprise," Judith called out, then turned, exposing the sleeping dog.

Japhia stopped, like she couldn't believe her eyes. Finally, the words trickled out, "For me?"

"Yes, dear, if you want her."

The look on Japhia's face left no doubt.

"I've missed having a dog, since Reggie ran away." She had been friends with both Elah and his dog. She knelt beside her saying, "Does she have a name?"

Judith smiled, "Up to you."

"It would be hurtful to Haniel to call her Reggie, besides that's a boy's name. How about Princess?" The dog opened her eyes and her tail began pounding the floor. Japhia reached out her hand, palm up, and slowly approached, "Good girl, good girl." The dog didn't even sniff her hand, but went immediately to licking.

Nodding her head, Judith declared, "I think Princess likes you."

Japhia began petting the dog, scratching her behind the ears, and ended nuzzling her head in the dog's neck. The color of Japhia's hair and the dog's fur were nearly identical. It was obvious, the two of them would become completely inseparable.

"Where did she come from?" Japhia was full of questions.

"She followed me home from the market."

"Is she house broken?" she inquired.

"Yes, she is," Judith was making this up as she went along. Every once in a while, she'd look to the dog for affirmation.

"Can she sleep in my room with me?" Japhia almost pleaded.

"We can try that and see how it works," Judith agreed, starting to enjoy this.

"How much do you know about dogs?"

"Well, we had Reggie for most of Elah's life." It was still difficult for Judith to mention his name to her.

Japhia whispered, "I think he'd approve," and she meant it.

Judith followed with, "I'm sure he would. Now, off to bed, the both of you."

Japhia got up and the dog followed suit, "Come on, Princess," and she headed towards her room. The dog padded along with her. After she had fallen asleep, Princess returned to Judith's room, where Judith sat in bed reading by candlelight.

Princess put her head on the bed. "I think that went well?"

"Yes, it did," Judith, said relieved. "I feel really good about this and am very grateful for the role you will have in Japhia's life. I was beginning to worry about raising her all by myself."

"You know, when you are worried, you can talk to Rayeh any time you want to, like he is just sitting here in the room with you, because he is that close," he spoke tenderly.

"And the creator of the entire universe wants to listen to me?" It was hard for her to believe.

"Not just listen, he wants to talk to you, talk with you. He loves you."

"It's just difficult to comprehend."

"But none the less true." He spoke with such confidence.

"Could I even meet him?"

"I think you already have," and he touched his chest, "met him here."

She smiled, "Yes, but sometimes the heart yearns for more."

Princess, the dog, smiled too, "Yes, I know the feeling. Well, let me see. I should be back before morning, but if Japhia comes looking for me, tell her that you just let me outside to do my business. Could you open the front door for me?"

Judith walked with him down to the front door and opened it to reveal a portal. The guard standing beyond the door looking down the road that led to the house was none the wiser. Then the dog walked through the portal and disappeared from view. Judith closed the door soundlessly, the guard still standing there, unaware of what had just transpired behind his back. She went back to her bed, blew out the candle, and went happily to sleep.

R'gal lounged at the table, no longer in his dog form, with Rayeh. These times with just the two of them were very special. Rayeh passed him the goblet he had just filled. "That seemed to go quite well."

"Yes, my heart is once again filled with hope," R'gal sighed.

"In a world rapidly going the wrong direction, it is refreshing to see a small ray of sunshine." Rayeh seemed hopeful too, "but there is lots for us to do. Are you ready?"

"Oh goodie, I love it when you say that," and R'gal laughed.

"Good, here's what I would suggest and I am pretty sure that all of those who are involved will go along with the plan." He smiled.

"Pretty sure?" R'gal was thinking, *"Here we go again."*

"You do know that I can hear your thoughts, R'gal," he stated matter-of-factly.

"Yes, sir…sorry," he apologized.

"Apology accepted. Now, here we go…" and Rayeh shared with him what was on his heart.

Chapter Thirty-Three
A Distant Relative

Princess was back just before sunrise, stepping through the portal into Judith's bedroom. When Judith's eyes opened, she stretched, and saw her there, "Is everything all right?"

"Yes, I brought someone with me," and Rayeh also stepped through the portal.

She drew the covers around her shoulders, momentarily afraid, then looked into his eyes. "Is this who I think it is?" she asked fearfully.

Rayeh responded, "I am!"

She practically fell out of bed getting to her knees before him, "My Lord!" She didn't even know how to address him.

"You can call me Rayeh, it is just a name. You know who I am."

She peeked up at him, "I have so many questions…"

"And we have all the time in the world, just not right now." He smiled, "The household is about to awaken and Princess needs to get back to Japhia's room, but you wanted to meet me in the flesh, as it were, so now you have. I look forward to our chats." He smiled again, turned, walked back through the portal, and it closed.

"We also have lots to talk about. Maybe tonight after Japhia goes to sleep?" Princess asked.

She was still a bit mesmerized, "Yes, I'd like that." Princess headed for Japhia's room.

Princess laid down at the foot of the bed just moments before Japhia opened her eyes. Japhia quickly looked for her and seeing her, tapped the bed for her to come up. Princess joined her on the bed and they snuggled for a bit. Japhia got up and went into the adjoining bath to complete her toilet and dress. Princess waited for her on her bed. Japhia returned dressed modestly, her hair combed, wearing the minimal makeup she always wore. She was ready for her day.

Princess followed her to the dining area, where Judith had set her a bowl of food scraps and another for water. Princess then lay at Japhia's feet until she had finished her meal. They spent the entire day together and Japhia's fondness for her grew and deepened. That evening, when Japhia finally drifted off to sleep, Princess went to Judith's room.

Judith did not employ any guards inside the house. One manned each of the doors, another the stable, and some walked the perimeter of the property. They worked in shifts releasing each other every four hours. Inside the house there were the servants and they all had some military training. Haniel had seen to that. They were skilled in hand-to-hand combat and the use of any weapon that was at hand, or any item that could be used as a weapon. Judith felt entirely safe.

She motioned Princess up onto the bed, who climbed up and sat beside her.

"That was difficult, having you here all day and not talking to you," she confided.

"You can talk to me. Japhia does all the time. I just won't answer." She put her head in her lap and Judith scratched her behind the ear without thinking.

She stopped, "I've never thought to ask, do you like being treated like a dog, scratched, petted…?"

"Actually, yes. I appreciate the signs of affection. It was somewhat different with Elah. When I was his tutor, he couldn't very well scratch me behind the ear, but I still knew he loved me. As a dog we were pals. It will be different when Japhia learns who I fully am."

"Should I tell her who you really are?" Judith feared her response to the ruse.

"Judith," Princess sought to calm her fear, "I am no less me as Princess. It is not a ruse, that would imply an intention to deceive. It is my goal to guard, protect, and befriend, and I can currently do that best as Princess."

Judith breathed a sigh of relief, "Thank you, that helps."

"Now, on to planning. Your sister has a distant relative who is soon coming to visit from the East, Jared by name. He is coming with his son, Enoch, who is quite a young man and destined to become a powerful influence for good. Japhia should meet him while they are here. You need to have a chat with your sister and let her divulge this information and issue you an invitation to join them." While this information was delivered dispassionately by a dog, there was also something wonderful that accompanied it.

"And you know this how?" She was intrigued.

"Our mutual friend," and Princess lifted her nose heavenward.

"Ah," she understood.

Thus was put into motion the plans that would introduce Japhia to Enoch, and what an introduction it was. It was designed as a small intimate dinner at Judith's sister's place.

That meant that there would be less than one hundred in attendance. There were close to one hundred who arrived during the course of the banquet. The expansive banquet hall was decked out in all of its glory, including the finest china from the east, a collection to which Jared had recently provided an expensive addition. Japhia was seated next to Enoch at the head table and they were waited on by the servants. The rest in attendance picked their food up off of the banquet table.

Enoch was not much for small talk, "Have you met the Creator of the universe?"

Japhia was a little shocked, "Not personally," and chuckled.

He smiled in return, "No, I'm quite serious."

Japhia still grinned, "How are you sure that he is not a she?"

He continued unfazed, "Because I have met him and he's not."

"Really," she realized he was being serious, "should I be offended that he is only male?"

"Oh, excuse me. He is not only male; he is much more than male. After all, he is the Creator, but he reveals himself in the form of a man, at least to me. That is why I refer to him in the male gender."

Japhia kept playing along, "And does he have a name?"

Enoch had a wonderful smile, "Many actually, but I call him Rayeh."

She was a little shocked again, "'Friend,' you call the Creator 'friend'?"

"I do, and I hope he calls me his friend." He picked up a goblet and took a drink.

She got serious and curious, "When did you meet him?"

"Ah," he paused as he remembered, "it was a little over a year ago."

"A year ago?" She was fascinated.

"Oh yes." He added, "He told me that I would meet you."

Japhia sounded startled again, "He told you this a year ago?"

"Oh, no," he had confused her and needed to make it right. "He told me about you while we were on the way here. We were traveling and one evening I went for a walk. My father worries about my safety when I do that, but he needn't. Anyway, I was walking under the stars and suddenly there he was beside me. It was funny, I wasn't startled at all. He was just there. I said, 'Hi,' and he put his arm around me and hugged me to him and said, 'It's good to see you.' I know he can always see me, but I knew what he meant. Then he continued, 'You're going to meet a very special woman on this trip. I think you will like her.' We talked about some other things, but that was all he said about you. And you know, he was right."

"About what, that you would meet me?" She pondered this.

"That too," and he paused for effect, "but also…that I would like you," and he looked deep into her eyes, "and I do."

Japhia started to blush, "Could you pass me the meat, please?" Their evening was very special.

That was the beginning of their relationship, their friendship that blossomed into a romance. Enoch stayed there, in their city, to begin a branch of his father's export business. He became a frequent visitor of Japhia at Judith's home. One evening as they were all lounging around the table after supper, Princess was stationed at her normal place near Japhia's feet, and Enoch addressed them all.

"Have you ever met an angel?" and he looked around the table. Princess lifted her head, ears forward to listen intently.

Judith cleared her throat, "My husband, Haniel, used to be an angel," she looked at Princess with concern.

"Used to be?" It seemed a question, but Enoch may have already known the answer.

She took a long drink, "Yes, a long time ago there was a rebellion in heaven. Lucifer, Raziel, Haniel and their armies were expelled from heaven and confined here to earth."

"That might explain it," Enoch continued.

"Explain what?" She wondered where this was going.

"Tell me some more first, if it isn't prying."

"Haniel and I had a son, Elah. He was an Ashereem, although he didn't belong to them. Elah slew an Ariel in single combat and then, while courting Japhia, he was slain by two others. My husband and another angel slew the two Ariel. My husband left me shortly after that and has his own house near the training grounds. Later Japhia came to live with me," she looked tenderly at Japhia, "like the daughter I never had. Elah's birth had made me barren."

"You said that your husband and another angel dispatched the Ariel. Was this Raziel or Lucifer or…" and he paused.

"No! It was an angel who was still an angel, not one of the 'fallen.'" It was becoming emotionally difficult for her to recall all of this.

"Do you know his name?" How could he ask all of this, yet still with such compassion?

Judith looked at Princess, "R'gal."

"Ah, that one," and Enoch also looked at Princess.

R'gal asked himself, *"Am I about to be exposed?"* and heard, *"Would you like him to stop?"* He thought, *"Yes,"* and almost said it out loud.

Enoch concluded with, "That would explain it."

"Explain what?" Judith's curiosity piqued again.

"Why this is such an interesting place. If spirituality were fragrances, there are a variety of them swirling all around and through this place. Don't get me wrong, your home is wonderful, a sanctuary, a beacon of light, all at the same time, but there are also lingering fragrances of what you have identified as the 'fallen' here and also the pure odor of sanctity that I would identify with those of the 'un-fallen' here too." Enoch took a long pull from his goblet. "I take it, you have met Rayeh?" It was less a question than a statement.

Japhia piped in, "Your friend who is the Creator of the universe?"

Judith was both surprised by the question and that Japhia knew about him, having not been party to Enoch's and Japhia's conversation that night, but she answered regardless, "Yes, I have met him."

"Perfect. I have a proposal. I'd like to take Japhia and her dog off your hands. I might as well do this in one fell swoop. I'd like to marry Japhia, if she'll have me." Japhia looked at him to see if he was serious. He was.

"Don't you think you should ask me first?" Japhia wasn't hurt, just caught off guard.

"Can I have some time to think about it?" Judith responded.

"Like I said, 'one fell swoop.' Let's all ask him," and he pointed upward.

"Now?" The girls asked in chorus.

"No time like the present," Enoch said confidently. Then he spoke to Rayeh as though he was in the room with them, "Well, Rayeh, what do you think?"

Judith heard him as though he stood next to her, *"This would please me very much."*

Japhia heard, *"The choice is obviously yours, but your marriage to Enoch would please me."*

Enoch heard, *"You rogue, are you trying to force my hand?"* To which Enoch responded in his head with a smile, *"Never, sir,"* and he heard, *"then proceed."*

R'gal heard, *"Sorry, sometimes Enoch rushes me a bit, but he knows me pretty well. I probably should have warned you. For that I apologize."*

"And…" Enoch left the rest unsaid.

"If you were to propose properly, I would accept," Japhia grinned.

"And you would have my blessing," Judith also grinned.

Enoch looked at Princess, "and the dog?"

R'gal nodded his head up and down.

"Then it's settled!" Enoch's confidence bloomed again.

"There is the matter of Japhia's parents," Judith interjected.

"Already covered," and Enoch's grin matched theirs, less the dog of course.

Enoch knelt in front of Japhia, "Will you be my wife?"

"Can I think about it?" she teased.

He leaned forward and kissed her tenderly, then leaned back, "Now?"

Her eyes were still wide with surprise and she spoke with difficulty, "Yes!"

PART FIVE
In The Days of Noah

Chapter Thirty-Four
Where Do We Go Now?

I'm sorry about there being no heads up before that meeting with Enoch at Judith's." It was evident in his voice.

"You know that I trust you implicitly," R'gal looked across the table at Rayeh.

"Yes, I do know that, without even being inside your head," and Rayeh smiled. "Working with Enoch," and he hesitated, "is complicated. He is human, remember, but the best one I've seen in a long time. The best by far."

"I do have some questions though," R'gal hesitated himself. "How long do I get to stay here? I do like not having to be a dog." They both almost laughed. "Enoch was about to tell Japhia about me. If it's possible, I'd like to do that myself."

"First answer, you can stay here a while. You know that time here and time there work differently. I can send you back to the spot you left with only moments having elapsed there." Rayeh grabbed a fruit, a deep purple one, and winked at R'gal as he bit into it. "I will also try and keep Enoch away from revealing your angelic identity, although Japhia is sure to ask him questions after that last conversation. Hopefully, she'll soon be too consumed with wedding plans."

"Will I no longer need to remain a dog when we move in with Enoch?" R'gal asked hopefully.

"There are some good things about being a dog, like getting lost in the woods for a while when you spend time here," Rayeh's grin broadened.

"But if you put me back moments after I left, does it really matter?" He still sounded hopeful.

"Ah, you were listening. Another benefit, you can be with her as a dog virtually all the time. That's difficult to pull off if you are another human." It was just information, but beginning to feel overwhelming.

"You're not trying to convince me to stay a dog, are you?" His hope was fading rapidly.

"You know that you always have a choice, but if you want my opinion, stay a dog. Well, you asked the question." He had only stated it as an opinion not as a command.

"Right, that's like saying, 'After reviewing all the possible outcomes, this one has the best chance of success' and thinking I'd choose something else." He shook his head wryly. "It's 'just' your opinion!" Then he added,"It would be funny, if it were funny," and smiled again. "So, when can I reveal to Japhia that I am an angel?"

"I'd probably wait until you were comfortably settled in Enoch's new home, sometime after the wedding." That was vague, but clear enough for now.

"And that's only your opinion?" R'gal grinned wider now.

"My studied, professional opinion, yes."

R'gal just shook his head and picked up his own deep purple fruit.

Because Japhia was the daughter of a prince, a princess in her own right, the wedding was an extravagant, opulent event. It was way more than either Japhia or Enoch really wanted, but it was taken completely out of their hands. There were almost as many of the fallen there as there were humans. Lucifer, Raziel, and a number of the Ashereem attended, complete with all the regular angels in rank-and-file order. They all had assigned seating, but that meant that Lucifer was at the head table. It was obvious that Lucifer did not like or approve of Enoch one bit and the feeling was mutual in Enoch's eyes. Haniel and Japhia's father gave her away while Jared and Enoch's brothers stood up for him. Fortunately, a priest conducted the ceremony or it might have been Prince Lucifer himself.

During the receiving line, Lucifer, as one of the first to greet the couple, shook Enoch's hand, to hear, "That was you in the Tree of Knowing in the Garden, wasn't it?" Lucifer dropped his hand like he'd been bitten, and maybe he had, but his attitude towards Enoch throughout the banquet bordered on open hostility. Haniel saw the exchange and although firmly entrenched in Lucifer's fold, found his respect of Enoch had grown significantly.

When Haniel took Enoch's wrist, he confided, "I don't know what you said to Lucifer, but I'm sure he earned it," and he looked him straight in the eye and winked.

After all the celebration, Enoch and Japhia were exhausted, but so happy to be in their own home. Princess slept outside the bedroom, ostensibly guarding the room from unwanted interruption, but even more appropriately engaged in prayer throughout the night. In the wee hours a portal opened before her, she got up, and walked through it to her favorite place with her favorite person.

Rayeh handed him, now in his human form, a goblet of wine. "I think we can all breathe a sigh of relief. Enoch's comment to Lucifer had me worried, but as usual, it went right home to where he had intended. He made no friend there, but he sharply defined the boundaries. It was easier than saying, 'Lucifer, you have no right to be here.' Or more appropriately, 'you have no place of authority here.' Enoch seems a bit of a loose cannon sometimes, but he is rarely off the mark."

R'gal was nodding in agreement with Rayeh's entire assessment of the situation, "And such a wonderful match for Japhia. They are so incredible together."

Rayeh continued, "You can inform them that they conceived a son last night and they will be very proud of him throughout his long life."

"So, he will live a long time? How long?" R'gal was just curious, being immortal.

"He will live longer on the face of the earth, than any other mortal man, but we will keep that part of the story just between us. His very name will be a testimony to my long suffering and loving kindness extended to all generations. No pressure, eh?" Rayeh chuckled.

"Yes," R'gal added his chuckle, "I can relate to that."

Sometimes it seemed like he spent a lot of his life outside of a room waiting for a baby to be born, because here he was again sitting at the feet of Enoch waiting for the delivery of his son. There had come an opportune moment, when he had the two of them alone, that Princess had been able to share with them that he was the archangel R'gal albeit in this form for their convenience. He had also shared with them that she was pregnant. At first, they hadn't believed it when he told them, but soon it became apparent. After that, they were more receptive to the news that at the appointed time they would receive a boy.

Their reverie was broken by the lusty cry of a newborn baby, but Enoch did not jump to his feet. He knew he must wait for permission from the midwife, even in his own home.

Finally, she joined them in the room. "You have a healthy son, my lord. You may go in to see them."

He looked at her pleadingly, "May I bring the dog?"

"It is your house, my lord. I would only ask that you keep her off the bed, as your wife is quite tired."

Together they quietly entered the bedroom, but Japhia was watching for them. "Your son, my husband," and she drew the blanket back from his little curly haired head. The child even turned towards them and smiled, cooing.

Princess looked about. They were alone, so she asked, "Do you have a name for the boy?"

Enoch smiled, "Although it will not be given formally until next week, his name will be Methuselah."

"'When he is gone IT will come,' an interesting name, does it have some special significance?" the dog asked.

"Yes, the Creator will extend his patience and loving kindness as long as Methuselah is alive upon the earth." His voice rang with prophecy.

"And when he is gone?" the dog questioned.

"There is more to come on that topic, I believe. So… stay tuned," Enoch added seriously, but with a grin.

Chapter Thirty-Five
The Righteous Line

The contrast became ever starker. Jared, Enoch, Methuselah and their families walked more closely with God, while the rest of the world declined rapidly into a moral abyss of debauchery.

Enoch began to go, almost daily, into the city and tell anyone who would listen, "Judgment is coming, the long-suffering patience of the Creator is almost at an end. Repent while you can. Turn away from your wrong. Let the Creator cleanse your heart and life. Come to him now while there is still time." With these and many other words he tried to reach them, but only a few responded, primarily women. Most of these left the city and moved out onto Enoch's property. He built a number of additional buildings, providing a place for them to live, and a large hall for them to gather for eating together, meetings, and worship. Many of the women and the few men worked in Enoch's vineyards, where he produced the finest wines in the entire province. Jared, his father, while still importing items from the East began to export Enoch's wines back to the East, until the proverb, "as fine as the wines of Enoch" became a byword for all things exquisite.

In time, Japhia delivered another son, then a daughter, two more sons, and another daughter. Now, while he waited for her to deliver twins, Enoch lounged at the table with the dog, Princess, waiting for news of the births. The sounds of labor had trailed off. He expected the cries of the babies, but there was nothing, only a deafening silence.

He turned to Princess, "Something's wrong," and the midwife stepped through the doorway, afraid to give the news. He sighed, "It's all right, I know something went wrong." She lowered her head, then actually knelt and began weeping into her hands. He got up, knelt with her, and wrapped his arm around her to comfort her.

When she finished sobbing, she forced the words out, "They are dead. There were complications. We could save none of them. I am sorry, I am so sorry," and she looked up through her tears.

He patted her reassuringly on the shoulder, "You did your best, I expected no less." He got up from his knees. "I need to see her." Patting his leg as he passed the dog, he called, "Come, Princess." They entered the room, a beautiful yet not opulent birthing room. So like Japhia, it radiated efficiency with a flavor of sanctity. Two servants still lingered, tidying up the place. "Please, leave us," he asked. They bowed as they left. Their eyes were red. They had obviously been weeping while trying to accomplish their tasks. When they were alone, Enoch spoke into the air, "Rayeh, do you want me to raise them from the dead?" He was stone cold serious.

A portal opened and Rayeh stepped through, walked up, put his arm around Enoch, and said, "There are a lot of things I could say, but they all seem to fall short. They are in a better place, which is true but of little comfort. The world is getting darker and more evil by the moment and I spared them from that, which is also true, but again of little comfort. The best I can do is say that I am very truly sorry and will walk with you through this grief and pain."

Enoch looked him straight in the eyes, "And that will be enough." He stepped to the bed, pulled the sheet down to just above her breasts. She had a child in each arm and none of the trauma shown on their faces. Even in the pales of death she looked radiant, as did her daughters. Maybe it was a trick of the light, more probably it was their purity shining through even in this darkest of moments. He kissed each child on the forehead, and lastly Japhia. He pulled the sheet back over them. "Princess, have you anything to say?"

R'gal looked up to Rayeh, "I'd like to stay with Enoch if I may?"

Rayeh nodded his agreement, "Of course."

When Enoch's oldest son, Methuselah, was grown, he thought they should branch out into olives. He shared the idea with Enoch, who concurred. They began purchasing orchards and soon were growing the best olives in the province. Enoch tasked Methuselah with the oversight of that portion of the business. It seemed like everything Methuselah put his hand to prospered, just as it had with his father. Methuselah married Jepheh, one of the women who worked in his father's vineyard. Enoch joked about Methuselah's courting of Jepheh, "You only wanted my best wine steward so you could make her a part of your olive oil business." It did provide an extra benefit to Methuselah, but came nowhere near explaining the truth. You just had to watch the two of them together to see it.

The wedding involved only their local families. While Methuselah, Enoch, and Jared did a thriving business with the cities around them, they kept themselves separate and apart from them socially, governmentally, and spiritually. For all the families who called Enoch's property home, it was a very special event that ended with the conception of another son in their long line of righteous men and women.

Lucifer moved to one of the larger cities. His eyes were fixed on controlling the entire planet and with his extensive network of spies it would soon be possible. He ignored Jared, Enoch, and their families, a terrible strategic error on his part.

On the day of his dedication, Methuselah's son was named Lamech and he followed Rayeh in every way, just like his father, grandfather, and great-grand father. In fact, his great-grandfather, Enoch, walked so closely with Rayeh that one day Rayeh said to him, "How would you like to go home with me to my house and see where I live?" Enoch was delighted. Rayeh took him there, never to return to earth. The world did not realize how much it would miss his restraining presence and fiery preaching of repentance, as it continued to run pell mell towards the abyss.

The portal opened and Princess padded through to become R'gal in his human form. He stood still a moment to regain his bearings. He had been a dog for quite some time on this last trip.

Rayeh was lounging at the table with Enoch. "R'gal, you know Enoch, although he may not recognize you in your human form." They nodded to each other.

"The world misses you dreadfully. Your family is a flickering candle in a vast and growing darkness. There is little holding the entire world back from its descent into the bottomless pit." Sadness tinged every word R'gal uttered.

Enoch smiled, "Yet as long as my children are alive, there is still hope. Methuselah still lives, yes?"

"Yes, I should be more optimistic, but even though I'm an angel, I am growing tired of all this evil," R'gal sighed deeply.

"You've heard the parable, 'It's darkest just before the dawn'?" Rayeh interjected. "Well, Lamech is about to have a son. He will be called 'Noah' which means 'rest,' for he will give us rest from all of that," and he gestured back towards the portal.

Rayeh spoke something he had been deliberating for a long time. "I too have grown weary of all this evil. Noah will be the last of the long-living ones. From now on, man's span upon the earth will be severely limited before he returns to the dust. Because evil has become so prevalent, I regret that I made man. I will blot him from the face of the earth, along with the animals, birds, everything that he has polluted. I am sorry that I made them all."

Enoch and R'gal were stunned speechless.

Enoch found his voice first, "And what of the righteous? There are still a few righteous remaining in my lineage."

Rayeh took a drink from his goblet. "True," he paused, "this will not happen tomorrow. I will not blot out the lives of any of the righteous. They will die naturally before I eradicate this disease." He paused again, "For now, R'gal, please go and attend the birth of Lamech's son."

That the righteous would not be destroyed by whatever Rayeh was planning seemed of some comfort to R'gal, yet he asked one question, "Do you think it's time I go back to being a Basenji? Some people are starting to notice that Princess has been around for a very long time."

"It is interesting that you should ask. I was thinking the same thing. I would probably change color again though. May I suggest white?"

R'gal turned into a white Basenji.

Rayeh smiled, "Perfect."

Chapter Thirty-Six
Lamech's Son

Lamech stroked the head of Rolf, who occupied the sofa with him. Princess had wandered off, never to return. In her place, a few days later, a stray white Basenji had showed up on their property. Lamech took him in and Methuselah named him Rolf. No one knew the dog's age. He seemed mature, but still spry. When Lamech first met him, he asked his father, "How old is Rolf?"

Methuselah laughed, "I really have no idea. He just showed up one day after Princess left."

"Didn't you find that…interesting? Maybe he is more than just a dog," Lamech laughed.

"Don't be silly," Methuselah smiled too. Still Lamech treated Rolf more like a human than a dog. And then one day Rolf spoke to him.

"You were correct, I am more than just a dog." Lamech should have been afraid, yet felt strangely at peace. "I am here mostly for your son."

"*How could he know that my child will be a boy?*" Lamech wondered. Lamech ventured cautiously, "How could you know that?"

"Let's just say that I have inside information." Rolf wished he could smile.

Lamech himself smiled, "A son," and believed Rolf. They waited, not speaking any more. Lamech could hear his wife's muffled cries and sobs of labor from the birthing room. Then, they stopped and were replaced by the lusty cries of a baby. Still Lamech and Rolf waited. They knew their place at this moment.

Finally, one of the midwives appeared, "My lord, come meet your new son."

He looked at Rolf and winked, "May I bring the dog?"

She shrugged, "It is your house, my lord."

They both got up and went to meet the boy who would be called Noah.

Noah expressed no interest in many typical boy things. His version of adventure was strolling through new parts of the forests that surrounded their home. He loved to search for and find new plants, fruits, vegetables, trees, and bushes. One day, as he was walking through the forest with Rolf at his side, out stepped a young man in the prime of life. Rolf barked, but did not growl. Noah should have been frightened, but on the contrary was intrigued by this young man.

The young man smiled, "Let me introduce myself. My name is Rayeh." Rolf was wagging his tail ferociously as Rayeh knelt and called, "Rolf, come here, boy." The dog practically leapt into his arms.

"You know my dog?" Noah was a little wary.

"Let's say, I knew his previous master," and he winked at the dog.

"You're not going to take him away, are you?" Now he was worried.

"Oh no, he is yours for as long as you still walk this ground," Rayeh assured.

"Good! It would be difficult to imagine life without him. He is my closest friend," Noah confided.

"And that relationship will continue, but there will be other close relationships." Rayeh paused, "I have someone I want you to meet." He pointed to a break in the trees that opened to a lovely meadow of short, cropped grass. In the middle of the meadow grew a single tree, the likes of which Noah had never seen, and below the tree, on her knees, a young woman appeared to be picking up some things off the ground. Noah and Rolf walked forward. Rayeh was no longer to be seen. Noah had perfected the art of walking with little sound so as not to disturb the animals as he explored.

He called out softly, "Good morning," although it was near noon.

She was not startled, but acted as if she had expected him. "Hello," her voice almost tinkled. Noah was shocked, she could have been Rayeh's twin sister. She continued, "My name is Naamah, and you are?"

Noah finally found his voice, "Noah, my name is Noah."

She looked off into the distance, "And he shall bring rest to those in this chaos, a new and fresh beginning."

"Excuse me?" Noah looked disoriented.

"Oh, I'm sorry, it just came to me like the words of a song. I should have sung it." Suddenly she did, and he was shocked to the very soles of his feet, nearly trembling.

He stuttered, "That was... precious," and he used the translation of her name.

"Why, thank you," and her disarming smile banished all else except a desire just to stand there and be with her.

He shook his head to clear it. It didn't help much. "What are you doing?"

She looked up into the tree, "Have you ever seen the likes of him?"

He had to admit, "No," and in his head, *"nor the likes of you."* He also wondered, *"Why did she refer to the tree as a 'he?'"* He asked her again, "What were you doing?"

"Oh, I'm sorry, I forgot that you already asked me that. I was walking through the forest, came to this meadow, saw the tree, and heard a voice. I know, that sounds a little weird, but it was the nicest voice. He said, 'Stop and collect some of the seeds from the tree. He's dropped them just for you.'" She paused, "You may wonder why I referred to the tree as a 'he'? Well, the voice did. So, I did too." She still knelt, "The answer to your question is, collecting seeds."

"Would you like some help?" he offered as he looked down at her.

"Yes, Noah, I would love that." Her face radiated another enchanting smile.

He knelt on the grass with Naamah and began picking up seeds and putting them in the pocket of his tunic. Rolf then nudged him, "Oh, I forgot to introduce you to my dog. This is Rolf." She held out her hand, palm up, and Rolf sniffed it then licked it. "I think he likes you." Rolf walked closer to her and she started scratching him. "Be careful, he'll let you do that all day long," and he laughed lightly. "So, do you know why you are collecting these seeds?"

"I think I might. There is a newly-plowed field between my brother, Tubal-cain's and Lamech's. I think I am supposed to plant them there," she shared.

He blurted out, "You're Tubal-cain's sister? I'm Lamech's son."

"Hmmm," she mused, "we're related, but from different mothers. I wonder why we have never met?"

"We'll have to make up for lost time," and he winked at her. They continued picking up seeds until their pockets were filled, then Noah asked, "When were you going to plant them? Could I help?"

"Tomorrow, and I would love the help." She stood.

"Great, I will bring my pocketful of seeds with me," as he too stood. He reached out his hand and they held hands for a moment. "I hope to see you tomorrow."

Slowly, and reluctantly, they both left and went to their respective homes.

Chapter Thirty-Seven
Naamah and Noah

The next morning Noah ate breakfast early and quickly completed his chores in order to present himself before his parents asking, "Is it alright if I go over to Tubal-cain's for the day?"

Lamech and Adah looked at each other, "Why are you going over to Tubal-cain's?"

Noah held up the sack of seeds. He also had the handle of a small hand shovel protruding from his pocket. "Naamah and I are going to plant some seeds." He had mentioned meeting Naamah the prior evening and seemed quite smitten with her.

His parents chuckled knowingly, then asked, "Where will you be planting these seeds?"

As though it were some great discovery, he shared, "Tubal-cain has plowed a field between his property and ours." Noah stood a little taller.

"And you asked him if you could use it for your seeds?" they inquired.

"Naamah was going to do that." He was feeling pretty grown up for his young age.

"And you are assuming an affirmative answer?" They smiled.

"Yup!"

"Then off you go," laughed Lamech.

"Be back for dinner," added Adah.

"Can I bring Naamah back with me?" he asked, looking just under his eyebrows.

Adah nodded her head, "If it's okay with her parents."

He was gone almost before she finished the sentence.

When he got to the field brandishing his hand shovel and bag of seeds, she was already there. The field had been plowed very well and in such a way as to facilitate their planting. He sat down on the grass next to her at the edge of the field and Rolf laid down at his feet.

"Do you have a plan?" his eyebrows raised.

She scowled a little, "Of course I do. Do you?" Then she smiled and his heart melted. Just then Rolf barked and looked behind them. There stood Rayeh.

"Good morning, Noah and Naamah," he said, smiling as usual.

Naamah's eyes opened wide, "That voice! You're my voice!" It was more a statement than a question.

His smile deepened, "Well, I am a bit more than just a voice, but yes, I asked you to collect the seeds."

Rolf spoke up, "This is Rayeh."

They stammered, almost in chorus, "The dog talks?"

Rolf continued, "Rayeh and I have been friends for a long time. You need to hear what he has to say."

Still smiling that infectious smile, Rayeh sat on the ground beside them. "You were looking for a plan. I have one that I think you will appreciate." They settled down to listen. "Do you know what kind of tree these seeds come from?"

Naamah began, "No, it is unlike anything I have ever seen before, but it is wonderful."

Noah nodded his head, affirming her words.

"It is a tree of gopherwood," Rayeh shared.

"You mean a gopher, like the small rodent, sort of like a squirrel?" At the word squirrel, Rolf's ears instinctively perked up.

"Well, a gopher is a small rodent, smaller than a squirrel, and without the bushy tail. Squirrels live in trees and bury seeds and nuts in the ground. Gophers burrow in the ground, digging tunnels, and find their roots and nuts in that process. Interesting side note: gopher tails are not bushy, although they may be fur-covered, and the ends of their tails are extremely sensitive. They use their tails to feel the sides of the tunnel when they are moving backwards. In fact, they can travel backwards almost as fast as they can run forward. But enough trivia."

"And what do these seeds have to do with gophers?" Noah asked for the both of them.

"Just as the gopher is a special kind of rodent, this tree is a special kind of tree, so I nicknamed it gopherwood. In point of fact, there is no other tree like it, and I want you to grow lots of them for a very special purpose." There, he'd said it.

"What kind of purpose?" Noah asked.

"That will have to wait, right now we need to do some planting." And that was that. "Naamah, I want you to plant two rows of seeds, one on each side of you, down the entire length of the field. Each seed needs to be about four cubits from another, the rows about four cubits apart, and each row staggered when compared to the next. So, for a gap on one side there is a seed on the other in that gap." Naamah knelt down, began planting, and Rolf walked beside her.

"You're not a dog, are you?" she asked him.

"I am a dog, but more than a dog. I am an angel sent to guard and protect you and Noah," Rolf whispered.

"And what exactly is an angel?" She was simply inquisitive.

"Well, I can't show you right now, out here in the open, but sometime soon I will show you. We are powerful spiritual beings that work behind the scenes for Rayeh."

"And what is special about Noah and I?" She liked the sound of the two of them together.

In his heart Rolf was frantically asking Rayeh for help, *"How much of this can I share?"* He moved on, "That you both are very special will have to suffice for now." He paused, "Would it help if I held the bag for you?"

"Why, yes it would," and she held out the bag by one of the straps that he grabbed with his mouth. She laughed, "And now you're going to claim we can't converse anymore because you have a bag in your mouth." His words were muffled and he wagged his tail furiously, nodding his head up and down.

Chapter Thirty-Eight
Planting and Watering

Rayeh and Noah walked to the center of the field.

"Noah, I want you to plant seeds in a circle ten cubits in diameter. Plant the seeds about four cubits from each other and only plant three-quarters of the circle. Then move out four cubits and plant another three-quarter circle circumscribing the first. Then move out a final four cubits and plant another circle."

"Yes, sir." Standing in the middle of the field, Noah made a mark in the dirt. He walked five cubits to the left and made another mark. He then walked ten cubits back right, across the center of his first mark, and made his final mark. He walked back to the center and set down his sack of seeds. He removed the rope belt around his middle and had Rayeh stand in the middle straddling the bag of seeds, as he played out the rope until he stood on the left mark. He held the rope to his chest and began side-stepping in a circle, keeping the rope taut between him and Rayeh. Rayeh nodded his pleasure, impressed at Noah's ingenuity. In this manner, he marked out the entire three-quarter circle, then picked up his bag and knelt with shovel in hand.

"Would you like some help?" Rayeh asked.

Noah was surprised, but responded, "You don't have a shovel."

"It's okay, the ground is pretty soft. Can I borrow your belt? And I'll need a handful of seeds." Still surprised, Noah handed him both.

Rayeh put the seeds in his pocket, tied a knot in the end of the rope, and another four cubits from it. He knelt on the ground at the beginning of the three-quarter inner circle, placed the one knot on the inner circle, moved out four cubits to the other knot, and planted a seed. Then he moved four cubits around the circle and did it again. Each seed was four cubits from its neighbor and four cubits from the inside circle.

About the sixth hour, some of Tubal-cain's servants brought them a light lunch. They lay on the grass that bordered the field, looking out on the beginning of a beautiful afternoon. The sky was a striking shade of blue, with a perfect sun, not too hot, but not too cold either.

Rayeh broke the silence, "It's hard to believe that the world is heading toward chaos and the darkness of the abyss on an afternoon such as this." A sadness echoed behind his words.

Naamah screwed up her courage, "Rolf says he's an angel. What does that mean?"

"He told you that?" Rayeh scowled at Rolf, the dog.

"And that the two of us are special." Here she grinned at Noah.

"Yes, you are special, and I have sent him here to protect you."

"A dog can protect us." She seemed unconvinced.

"Remember, he's not just a dog. He's an angel, and when the time is appropriate, he will show you what all that means. Again, that will have to do for now. This is the time to continue planting." Over the next two days they finished seeding the entire field. Rayeh had told them the dirt of the field was ideal for the growth of the trees. The only thing lacking would be enough water. Each morning, as they knew, the ground would be covered with dew. This facilitated sustaining normal growth, but proved insufficient to allow new life to fully germinate during the first month.

The next evening while now having supper at Tubal-cain's house, Noah and Naamah were discussing the lack of water with him when he responded, "I think I have a solution for your water problem. Come back in the morning and I'll show you."

Noah finished his breakfast and chores early and made his way quickly to Naamah's home with Tubal-cain. A servant escorted him and his dog directly to Tubal-cain's shop, where Naamah already stood waiting. She took him inside. In all the times he had visited, he had never been taken to the workshop. It was a place of mystery and awe. A craftsman of metal that bordered on art, an inventor of tools and machinery, Tubal-cain worked in and around all manner of wondrous things. Noah stopped at the door, amazed.

Tubal-cain laughed, "You can come in, just don't touch anything without asking. Some of them," and he gestured all around him, "are dangerous and could unintentionally hurt you." He waved them in further, "It's over here. I call them my 'mobile irrigators.'"

Noah saw a metal barrel, affixed atop a stand on a cart about a cubit above the ground, with copper tubing extending from a single faucet near the barrel's bottom. The tubing would direct water to the back and out to each side. At the end of each tube a bulb full of holes would turn the water into spray. There were two of the odd contraptions side by side. Noah wondered if Tubal-cain was always this jovial in his workshop or just proud of his creation.

"Noah, how good are you with horses?" Tubal-cain asked.

"I'm pretty good with dogs," and he looked at the doorway where Rolf sat, wagging his tail in confirmation.

"Well, if you'll take one cart, I'll take the other and we'll go hook them up to some horses and take them to the field of trees. I know, it's more a field of soon-to-be-called trees," and he chuckled at his own joke.

They had no trouble with the horses at all. Noah wondered if Rolf had a word with them before the humans got there. At the field stood a huge barrel already filled with water. All of this appeared to have been designed and fabricated exactly for this purpose. You drove a mobile irrigator up to each side, where a pipe ran from the huge barrel and over to the irrigator's barrel. Two servants then turned the hand-cranks that pumped water from the huge barrel into the irrigators. That completed, they positioned the irrigators at the end of field's rows two and five. This would allow them to water six rows during each pass. Tubal-cain must have calculated the flow from the irrigators compared to the length of the rows to allow a single pass to water the entire length of the field. At the end of the field, they spied another huge barrel and two more servants.

They positioned the horses and the irrigators, and as they began to walk, the servants opened the irrigators' faucets. The spray perfectly covered the six rows as they walked along and after only a few steps, Noah composed a song in his rich tenor voice,

We collected the seed that he had shown us,
And planted them per his own instruction,
And watered them with Tubal-cain's devices.
We did exactly what he had told us,
And followed the letter in his direction,
To cover the field in exactly six row slices.
We may plan, and we may water,
But he commands the increase.
We will stand, and will not falter,
Until our forest grows in peace.

Noah repeated the chorus for Naamah to learn and then repeated the verse. She joined him in the chorus and by the third time around they blended in harmony, her sweet alto with his rich tenor voice. They watered the field of trees every day for the next month and were rewarded with tender little shoots growing to nearly a cubit in height by the end of the year.

Naamah and Noah continued to be nearly as inseparable as Noah and Rolf. Even though they had to spend evenings apart because they didn't live together, yet they often found ways around that too. They often invited one another to each other's home for supper.

Chapter Thirty-Nine
More Than Just Trees

One morning Naamah walked out to her field to find, in the middle of what would one day become an entire grove of gopherwood trees, a bench of tightly grained, dark, rich, red wood. On the left-hand side of the bench was carved her name. On the right-hand side sat Noah. He stood revealing the name 'Noah' carved beneath where he had been sitting. He reached out his hand, she took it, and they sat down on the bench together.

"My father brought back a carpenter from his last trip. I have been apprenticed to him." He paused as if for effect. "This is my first project, a gift to us and our friendship. May it become something more than just a friendship, just as this," and he gestured around them at the trees that were now as tall as they were, "is more than just a field of trees."

Ten years later, the trees were ten cubits tall and the canopy of the grove over-shadowed the bench, shielding it from the heat of the day. They still often met for lunch at the bench. Noah was now a full carpenter in his own right. He had to work each day, but he still ate lunch and a quick walk would take him to the field of trees. He made all kinds of things now, from farm implements to household furniture. He had made quite a name for himself with the beauty and excellence of his products. This noon he was late for lunch. Naamah sat on the bench waiting for him with cups and a pitcher of cold water.

She sighed, wondering, *"This is unusual, he's not usually late for anything."*

Suddenly, he was there, smiling like he knew a secret. He had brought no basket of food. *"Was she supposed to have brought enough for them both today?"* she questioned herself.

As if reading her mind, he answered, "No, I'm not particularly hungry today." That was unusual too. He almost laughed at her surprised look. "I stopped off at the house and spoke with Tubal-cain before I came. That's why I am late."

She furrowed her brow, "Why did you need to talk to him?"

He pulled his hand out from behind his back. She hadn't realized it had been hidden there. In his palm lay an intricately carved wooden ring. "I needed his permission before asking you to be my wife." Tears glistened in her eyes as he asked, "Will you be my wife?"

She stood shakily, he stood confidently, "Yes," she whispered as a tear finally ran down her cheek and they embraced.

It took Noah an entire year to build them a house and a wood shop at the end of the field of trees. They held a small family wedding in the grove under the canopy of the gopherwood trees and when the festivities concluded, Noah took his new wife to their new home and conceived the first of their three sons: Shem, Ham, and Japheth.

Chapter Forty
The End of All Flesh is Before Me

R'gal and Rayeh lounged at their favorite table of refreshments. Rayeh looked pleased, "Your time as a dog is at an end."

"Really?" R'gal chuckled softly, "When I return here, it is often difficult for me to stand on my hind legs."

"You had better get used to it again. Noah is about to embark on one of the greatest building projects of all time." Rayeh raised a goblet, "To Noah!"

R'gal raised his too, "Yes, to Noah!"

On the twenty-fifth anniversary of their wedding after the evening meal, Noah and Naamah walked out to the bench where he had asked her to marry him. They found Rayeh sitting in the middle of their bench.

"Congratulations! I see things are going well. Even in a world that has gone mad you are able to provide a little corner of heaven on earth. I am very happy for you. This," and he gestured around, "is a tribute to what two young people can do by simply following me."

He patted the bench on either side of him. They sat, one on his left, and one on his right. Noah began, "Thank you! Serving you, following you, it is our greatest pleasure." He smiled at Naamah, "Well, one of our greatest pleasures,"

Naamah continued, "We are truly, wonderfully, blessed." She spoke with deepest sincerity.

Rayeh became quite solemn, "The time has come for the greatest adventure of your entire lifetime. Everything until now has led up to this."

"If this is such a great adventure," asked Noah, "then why are you so solemn?" added Naamah.

"I have grown weary of all this evil. You, Noah, will be the last of the long-living ones. From now on I will begin to limit man's time upon the earth." It seemed that even all of the night sounds had gone silent. "I regret that I made man." Noah and Naamah were almost afraid to breathe. "I will blot him out from the face of the earth, along with all the animals, the birds, everything that creeps upon the face of the earth. Man and his evil has polluted them all." A tear trickled down Rayeh's cheek. "But you, Noah, and your family, have found favor in my eyes. You, I will spare." Noah and Naamah breathed a sigh of relief. "I want you to build an ark."

"A…what?" Noah asked.

The solemnity lifted a little, like the sun beginning to peek out from behind a hill. "Remember when you would go on a picnic down by the river? Sometimes after lunch you would take the empty picnic basket, put it in the river and watch it float down the river for a while?" They both nodded. "You are going to build a very large basket, well, box of gopher-wood. That is why we grew the field of trees."

"How large a box?" Noah began to smile.

Rayeh himself smiled and the sun came back out in full strength. "Three hundred cubits long, fifty cubits wide, and thirty cubits tall."

Noah and Naamah looked at each other, "You're kidding?"

"Nope." Rayeh was enjoying this part. He continued "and it will have a roof over all of it, a large door in its side, and three decks: lower, middle, and upper. You will also make many individual rooms inside of it, and cover it inside and out with pitch." He looked at their bewildered faces and added, "I will teach you how to make the pitch."

Noah's eyebrows raised, "Why are we building this very large box?"

Rayeh turned solemn again, "I will destroy everything in whom is the breath of life by a flood."

"A what?" Noah interrupted, dumbfounded.

"Water will fall from the skies," Rayeh began.

"How is that going to happen?" Noah interrupted again. "It has never happened before."

"Never mind, just listen." Rayeh was not angry. "Everything is about to change and water will fall from the skies. The fountains of the deep will spew forth water, until the entire earth is covered in it. There will be no more land and everything will drown in the water except those kept safely in the ark. The ark will float upon the waters, like a basket on the river." He took a deep breath. "Of every living thing, you will bring two of them into the ark, both a male and a female, of the birds, of the animals, of everything that creeps upon the earth. One of each species. You shall keep them alive in the ark until the water recedes. That is why there will be so many rooms, for all the creatures, and for the food that you will need to store for them and for yourselves. You, your sons, and their wives will be the only humans on the ark."

Naamah, concerned, spoke up, "But what of our parents, grandparents, their families, all our relatives?"

"They will all have died before the flood, except Methuselah. He will be the last one to die. Remember the meaning of his name, 'When he is gone, it will come?' Now you know the meaning of the 'it' in his name. It is the flood. And I will establish my covenant with you and all on the ark who will build a new beginning." Rayeh chuckled, "I have one more anniversary present for you." Rolf came and sat before them. "He has many names: R'gal, Reggie, Rolf, but now he will become Regem," and the dog transformed before their eyes into a fit, mature man, who still seemed familiar even though no longer a dog. Rayeh chuckled again, "And he's almost as good a carpenter as you are, Noah." Rayeh stood, stepped away from the bench, and patted Regem on the back as he passed by him into an open portal which closed behind him.

Noah and Naamah were still in shock. Regem stepped forward and held out his hand to Naamah. She placed hers in his and he brought it to his lips to lightly kiss it.

"My mistress," and he smiled, "I guess I could have licked it," which broke the tension. He reached out and grasped Noah's forearm, "Should we go home? Tomorrow, we begin planning on how to build this ark." Regem chuckled, "And I'd appreciate sleeping in a bed rather than on the floor."

They all laughed. "I think we have just the place," chuckled Noah.

Chapter Forty-One
Beginning the Plan

Regem was up before the crack of dawn. One of the servants found him in the sitting room, at a writing desk, making a list. "May I get you something hot or cold to drink, sir?" she asked.

He smiled at her warmly, "I don't believe we have met. I am Regem. I will be working with Noah." Of course, he knew her, but only as Rolf the dog and not as the man Regem.

"Ah, yes, the Master spoke of you last night. I am Juniel," and she returned his smile.

"Juniel," and he paused, having said her name fondly, "Mistress Naamah speaks very highly of you. In fact, she doubts very much if she could run this household without you."

Juniel blushed. "Something to eat or drink?" she stammered as Noah walked in.

"Ah, Regem, already flirting with my staff?" he joked.

Regem winked at Juniel, who blushed more deeply. "I was considering it," as he faced Noah, then turning back to

Juniel, "One of your mint teas from the East would be wonderful. Thank you."

"What are you working on before breakfast?" Noah asked as he approached the writing desk.

Regem looked around to assure that they were alone. "You don't realize it, but I was the first animal to meet Adam when he named all of them. I make quite a majestic black stallion," he said mockingly proud, then he looked wistfully off into the distance. "That was my first meeting with a female. Rayeh made quite a fetching mare for me to meet Adam with." He shook his head to clear his thoughts, "So I know all of the original animals, birds, and so on and thought that a list of them all would help us plan how you will house them on the three decks of the ark."

"What a splendid idea! And I thought you were just here for the manual labor," and they both smiled to each other.

"For instance," and he took on a scholarly tone, "there are many breeds of dogs nowadays, but we will only need one pair of one breed on the ark. Now, I have been two of the breeds myself, one as Rolf, and one many years ago as Reggie. So, I thought I could help you pick the best one. Does that sound okay?"

"It does, it does, indeed. Ah, here's your tea," and Juniel stepped into the room, up to the desk, and set a brimming hot cup of tea carefully beside his list.

As she stepped away, he called her name, "Juniel." She turned back to him and he winked again, "Thank you." Flushing red, she retreated from the room.

Noah shook his head, "Well, I think you have made a friend there. She seemed pretty sweet on Rolf too, but don't expect her to scratch you behind the ears any time soon." Noah pulled up a chair next to him.

They spent the entire morning on the large animals for the lower deck. It seemed to make the most sense to have the most weight lower in the ark. The process uncovered a number of interesting questions. For instance, "Could Rayeh arrange for all the animals to be young and thus smaller?" Regem would have to ask him. Another, "Would the animals all be friends during the voyage?" That would make the lines of separation easier. "Could some of the animals sleep during most of the voyage?" That would drastically reduce food consumption. Another, "How would we get them all to where the ark would be built and then on the ark?"

Noah asked, "Is there any possibility that he could spare some more angels to help with the production of the lumber for the ark, and the ark's actual fabrication?"

Regem thought a moment, "Well it won't hurt to ask." They were called to lunch, but Regem declined, "You know I don't really need to eat to live. It's more to blend in, although I do enjoy it. I'll go have a chat with Rayeh."

As Noah stood, he joked, "You must metabolize fluids differently too. If I consumed as much tea as you have had this morning, I'd be floating." Noah smiled, "Or do you just like to have Juniel popping in from time to time?"

Regem raised his eyebrows as he stood, winked, and walked to the front door and into a waiting portal.

Chapter Forty-Two
Questions and Answers

Rayeh handed him a goblet as he emerged from the portal's other side, "Unless you have already had enough to drink." He turned back to the table and R'gal winked at his back. "I saw that."

"Wow, nothing gets by you, does it?" and they both laughed.

"So, how's the planning going?" he asked.

"You already know the answer to that. You know everything," R'gal returned.

"My oh my, do we have an attitude today?" At least Rayeh was grinning, "If you want to play that game, why didn't you just ask me from there? Why come here? I know," he paused, "you like to see my smiling face."

"I'm sorry, I guess this project is already showing me all that I don't know rather than what good I am going to be able to do," R'gal apologized.

"Who else knows all the animals by name? You were there. Of course, you are helping. So where would you like to start?" he said encouragingly.

"Could you arrange for all the animals to be young and small?" he ventured.

"That's a great idea, I'll do it."

"Could the animals be friends for the duration of the voyage?"

"Another great idea, consider it done."

"Now I think you're patronizing me," R'gal sighed.

"Nope! Not at all, go on."

"Could they sleep during the voyage?" and he looked up into Rayeh's eyes.

"That one is a little more difficult. Birds, for instance, don't have a good way to store food. They need to remain light to fly, but with many of the others we could probably pull it off. They would have to eat and store the food as fat for quite a while before you set sail, and it would compete against your young, small, and light request, but I think we can strike a balance."

"How are we going to get them all to the ark and on the ark?" This one really puzzled R'gal.

Rayeh took a drink from his goblet and refilled it. "There are differing levels of miracles. Why couldn't I just have them walk through portals from where they are right before I flood the earth, or to a place after I have flooded earth? But where would be the fun in that? You see, the ark is the portal. It will stand there being built for one hundred and twenty years as a testimony to my grace and mercy. Calling to the rest of the world, as Noah himself will do, 'Repent, repent, there is still time…' but they won't repent, sadly. Oh, and forget that I mentioned the one hundred and twenty years number." He chuckled.

"A hundred and twenty years, that's how long this is going to take?" That didn't sound like relief in his voice, more like resignation.

"You're supposed to be forgetting that number," Rayeh reminded him.

"Why so long?" he sighed again.

"Noah is the last of the 'long-living-ones'. From now on one hundred and twenty years will be the total lifespan of an individual. I will extend grace for each person's entire lifespan, then comes the judgment." It was beginning to make more sense.

"And the ark is the portal between the old and the new?"

"Yes, the bridge between the old and new and a symbol of my provision through even the most difficult of times." There was a finality to the way he said it that would probably make the labor seem less like 'work'.

"And getting them all to the ark and on it?" He was back to the other questions.

"I may lend you a few angels to act as shepherds just before that final day." He paused reflectively, "Angels as shepherds, I like the sound of that." He smiled at something else he must have been thinking about.

"And loaning us some other angels for the production of the lumber and fabrication of the ark itself?" he asked hopefully.

"Nope," he said lightly, "you are my only angel aid on that point. This is a task for man," and he smiled broadly, "and woman. I think you will be surprised how helpful the women are going to be." He paused, "and don't think your flirting with Juniel has gone unnoticed," and Rayeh laughed outright while R'gal blushed. It seemed only fair.

Noah had a fire pit in the back yard. Regem sat before the fire, staring into its dying embers. Juniel walked out from the house and stood beside him until he noticed her. He had wondered what that wonderful smell was. *"Why do women always smell so nice?*" he thought as he turned towards her, "Juniel, how long have you been standing there?"

"Not very long, my lord," she said demurely.

"Juniel, I'm not your lord. That would be Noah. I am just a friend of the family." He stopped and looked up into her eyes, smiling, "And your friend too, I hope."

She had a goblet of chilled wine in her hand which she held out to him, "I thought you might want…"

"And you were right." His smile deepened. "At what time do you finish your chores for the evening?"

Her dimples deepened, "I am already finished. I just thought that you might like the wine," and she lowered her head.

"And as I said, you were right." He patted the chair next to him, an invitation. It seemed that Noah had made a lot of chairs. Rarely did anyone just lounge around on cushions at his home. She sat. "Can you keep a secret?" She nodded and he continued, "What do you know about angels?"

She looked off into the fire, "Only what we have been taught. That Rayeh made them before he made man and they help him rule the universe."

"And why did he make man?" Regem asked her.

"To help him rule the earth, but we have messed things up," she replied sadly.

Regem too looked off into the fire, "Yes, and the world is getting worse and worse, and worse." He looked at her and caught her eye. He reached out a hand and she took it. "This place that Noah has built," and he looked around him, "is one of the few exceptions in the whole known world." She nodded in agreement. He let go of her hand almost reluctantly. "Do you know what an angel looks like?"

Her smile returned and she shook her head, "No! I don't believe that I have had the pleasure of meeting one," and her smile deepened, including the dimples.

"It is said that they are eight cubits tall, have wings like a bird, and can fly. Had you heard that?" She nodded again. "Would you find that terrifying?"

She looked back into the dying fire. "Probably," she stated matter-of-factly.

"Did your teachers also tell you that they can appear in different forms?"

She quickly looked back into his eyes, "At least the fallen ones, if I understand correctly."

He looked deeply into her eyes, "The fallen ones were in the form of men when they created the Ashereem. They are now confined to the form of men, but the un-fallen are not, they are different." He was looking for something in her eyes and trying to listen to Rayeh at the same time. "You acknowledged that you could keep a secret. I assume that means that I can trust you with one." She nodded again while retaining his gaze. "Place your hands in your lap." She did. "Close your eyes." Again, she did. "Take a deep breath in, and then slowly exhale." She slowly inhaled and then exhaled. "Open your eyes." There on the chair where Regem had sat, now sat Rolf.

Startled, she exclaimed, "Rolf? We thought you had left us!" She was excited and a little puzzled, and looked around for Regem.

She heard the words, "Juniel, I am both Regem and Rolf." She sat back, startled. "It's all right, I won't bite." His tail was wagging furiously, "Close your eyes again." Reluctantly she did. "You can open them." She opened her eyes slowly. Regem sat before her again, "I am an angel. There, now you know my secret."

She stammered, "Why are you telling me this?" somewhat afraid of the answer.

Regem looked back to the embers, "Because I like you and I believe that you like me, but you must know at the outset of our relationship that we can never be more than friends."

Her smile returned and she reached out her hand to him. As he took it, she declared, "and that will be wonderful enough," while she frantically tried to remember if she had ever kissed him as a dog.

He broke her reverie with, "This must remain our secret," and she nodded her assent and squeezed his hand as she brought it to her heart.

Chapter Forty-Three
Division of Labor

Regem had returned from Rayeh with the answers to their questions. Some were good news, others not quite so good.

"What? No other angels will be sent to help us? How will we ever complete this task?" Noah responded anxiously.

"Rayeh seems confident we can do all of this 'in house' and in the amount of time required." Regem tried to sound confident.

"And how long have we got to pull off this monumental building project that includes producing all the materials, stockpiling the food stuffs, and so on and so forth?" Noah seemed unconvinced.

Regem smiled sheepishly, "As long as Methuselah lives. Pray that he lives a long, long, time." Together they scratched out some drawings of the potential ark, complete with as much information as they currently knew. They would present it that evening to all the family, after supper.

They sat around one of Noah's tables, in chairs he had designed and constructed himself. Noah sat at the head, with Naamah around the corner to his right. Around on the left sat Japheth and Shem, next to Naamah sat Ham, and opposite Noah sat Regem. The dishes were cleared away and all that remained were goblets and pitchers of wine.

Noah began, "We all know how wicked the world has become with such corruption, violence, perversion, that it's hard to believe it could get any worse. Rayeh has spoken to me. I know, that sounds a little melodramatic, but still, it is true. He said it has gotten so bad that he is sorry he made man. Therefore, he is going to destroy everything in which there is the breath of life: mankind, animals, birds, creeping things, all of it." Noah took a deep breath as he filled his goblet.

All of their mouths were open wide with surprise, except Namaah's and Regem's. Ham finally found his voice, "How is he going to do that, destroy everything?"

After taking a long drink, Noah continued, "He will open the windows of heaven and water will fall from the sky. He will open the fountains of the deep and water will gush forth from there also. There will be so much water that it will cover everything and all will die, except those who escape in the ark."

Shem spoke this time. "The what?"

It was Regem's turn. "You know how sometimes on holiday at the river you have floated a basket in the river?" They all nodded. "We're going to build a very large basket." He put the sketches on the table. "It will house the selected birds, animals, and you, for Noah has found favor in Rayeh's sight. The ark will carry you safely through the flood to repopulate the earth. It is a chance for a fresh new start."

Japheth spoke, "And the materials to build this 'large basket'?"

Ham wondered out loud, “Where will these materials come from?”

Noah smiled, “You’ve heard the story of how I met your mother?” Naamah looked away as she blushed.

The three boys almost spoke in chorus, “She was picking up seeds from the gopherwood tree.”

“And we planted them together,” Noah continued, “and they have now grown into fine trees themselves. Rayeh has provided those trees for our basket,” and he chuckled.

Regem began again, “We will need to turn the trees into planks,” and he put another set of sketches on the table. “Ham, we are going to construct a mill to make the planks, using a large circle saw that you will fabricate. Japheth, you have horses trained to turn the mill that grinds our flour?” Japheth nodded. “You need to train another set to turn the gears and belts that will power the plank saw.”

They began by building the mill just north of the field of gopherwood trees. That way, they didn’t have to haul the trees very far. They would stockpile the lumber on the other side of the mill where they had just removed the trees, for that is where they would construct the ark, using the trees they had not harvested as scaffolding and supports for the ark. Regem gave them the numbers for all the birds and animals they would be bringing, along with estimates of the kinds and quantities of food they would need to accumulate. He did all this without ever having to reveal that they had one hundred and twenty years to accomplish the task. They did ask him, “Do you know when the flood will occur?” and were satisfied when he replied, “It will not come as long as Methuselah is alive. He is the visible expression of the extent of Rayeh’s grace and mercy.”

Japhia's granddaughter, Ereveem, had married Jubal. Jubal was a master of music and inventor of all manner of stringed instruments. One of his daughters, named Taphilla, whose voice could stop a wild beast in its tracks, married and had two daughters: Mashal and Meshkel. People said that when the two of them sang in harmony, the stars would stop in their course to listen. Mashal and Meshkel met Noah's two sons, Ham and Shem. The two men were totally mesmerized by Mashal and Meshkel singing, smitten as it were, and soon made them their wives.

Japheth, on the other hand, fell in love with Rayneh, one of Adah's grand-daughters and in due time he made her his wife. This completed Noah's family: his wife Naamah, sons Japheth, Shem, Ham, and their wives Rayneh, Mashal, and Meshkel. Now the work could begin in earnest.

Sitting around the table, they were almost too tired to eat. To keep up their strength, they ate anyway. The least tired of them seemed to be Regem, but then he had been directing the labor, when not actually involved in all of it.

Noah turned towards Regem, "How thick will the planks need to be? Rayeh gave us the basic design, but not a lot of the details."

"We can just ask him," Regem responded matter-of-factly.

Noah looked to the empty chair that was always left at the end of the table for a guest and asked, "What should be the dimensions of the planks for our," he paused and smiled, "basket?"

Shem looked quizzically at the end of the table, "I just saw a picture of a rather nice looking home, sitting peacefully on a hill."

"Ah, and what did it look like the dimensions of the planks used to build it were?" smiled Regem.

Shem smiled in return, "About ten cubits long, a span wide, and two fingers thick, I think."

Noah again looked towards the end of the table. "Is that the size we should start with?"

Shem spoke again, nodding his head up and down, "Yes, that is it."

Chapter Forty-Four
Beginning of the Labor

They had completed the entire lumber production process. This included the wagons to haul the tree trunks from where they felled them to the plank saw conveyor. They were picked up off the wagons with a crane and placed onto the conveyor. The conveyor delivered the trunks to the saw, where they were cut into span-high logs and then recut into two-finger-width planks. Another conveyor delivered the planks to the storage area.

Meanwhile, Noah and Regem designed the keel beam, the ribs, and the beams to support the bottom floor of the ark. They felled some trees and cut them into two-cubit lengths. These they used to line the entire length of the field where the ark would be built, about two cubits apart, and upon which they lay the keel beam. They attached the initial supports to the keel beam, and the planks that formed the floor to them, then the ribs up the side. It was long hours of back breaking work and sometimes they were so exhausted they could barely eat the evening meal.

Then one morning Mashal and Meshkel joined the men, along with their mother, Taphilla. She had brought with her a fiddle and as the whine of the saw began to fill the air, she added the harmony of her fiddle, and the women began to sing:

The tree gave us its seeds, which we planted in a field
To which we added water, while you provided sun to shine,
Till seedlings we had plenty, the ground expressed your glory
Becoming trees of unique beauty, tall enough, and just in time.

We're cutting trees and shaping them into the boards we need
Creating planks of lumber from the gopherwood
We're planing them and making them, a labor of our hands
Constructing from the forest, your promised ark of safety.

The world grows darker every day, till men can hardly see
While violence grows more evil, injustice spawning hate
More immorality, selfishness abounding signs of greed
Till chaos covers everything, until it is too late.

And yet we labor joyfully, creating something never seen
To sail upon a flood of waters that before has never been
To save us all from judgment swift, both animals and men,
The birds and every creeping thing, beginning new again.

So mesmerizing was the singing that the men might have stopped to listen, but actually it had the opposite effect. They doubled down to work even harder, their labor itself harmonizing with the singing. After the women sang it a second time, the men joined in on the third, even improvising some verses of their own. The day passed quickly and much more lightly than the others. They were ravenous for supper and slept that night like babies. The days continued to progress in song with differing instruments from time to time and one or more of the women to lead the first verses. Some have gone so far as to say that the ark was built by song, but it was at least song that helped its building go more easily and quickly.

Then there was the pitch. Their first reaction had been, as usual, "The what?" When Rayeh had said to coat the inside and the outside of the ark with it, at that time they had no idea what he had been talking about. Again, one evening as they sat around the dinner table, though no longer exhausted because of the help the singing provided, Ham broached the topic.

"Father, you told us that Rayeh wanted us to cover the inside and the outside of the ark with pitch. Should we ask him what he means?"

Noah looked towards the end of the table, "You want us to cover the inside and the outside of the ark with pitch. How do we do that?"

It was Shem who responded, "Huh, the pitch is the sap of the gopherwood tree, collected, and boiled with the charcoal left over from the lumber scraps we are burning. Then we sort of paint it on the inside and the outside of the ark as we build it. I guess I better get started on that tomorrow so that we don't get too far ahead of ourselves in the assembly process."

The next morning Meshkel accompanied Shem to the forest. She was humming a cheerful little tune as they walked hand in hand among the trees, far enough outside of the area that they thought would be part of those harvested for their lumber. Shem had brought a bag of tools along with them. It hung over his shoulder as they strolled among the trees. He had dreamt last night about the process of harvesting the sap from the trees. It consisted of boring a hole deep into the tree, then inserting a straw into the hole that would direct the sap out of the tree and into a bucket that hung from the straw. They both pulled small wagons filled with small buckets about four fingers in diameter.

For some reason it seemed almost a desecration to bore a hole into one of the trees. He wasn't sure why that was any different than cutting one down, but it seemed so. He finally stopped in front of a tree just as Meshkel ended her tune.

He looked at the tree and asked tentatively, "Are you the one?" It was if he received the response, "Yes, and these, my brothers and sisters in this part of the forest, willingly provide you with what you need." He looked at Meshkel.

She responded, "I heard it too. He is the first of these," and she gestured to the trees around them.

He set down the sack, removed the drill, and handed the first straw to Meshkel. He drilled a hole about chest high and about six fingers deep. By the time he inserted the straw and hung the bucket on the few fingers of it left protruding, the sap had already begun to drip. They moved to the next tree, and the next, and the next, until they ran out of buckets. When they went back to the first bucket, it had stopped dripping, being nearly three-quarters full. They collected all of the buckets and returned to where the ark was beginning to be assembled. Outside of the plank mill there was a pile of scraps of the trees from the milling process and a fire pit where they were being burnt. Next to it they had constructed another smaller pit to be used in the production of the pitch. They hung a caldron over it, into which they dumped the twenty-four buckets of sap.

Now, how much charcoal to add? He reached out his hand, she took it, and they both closed their eyes. When they opened their eyes, he held up two fingers and said hesitantly, "Two buckets of charcoal?" She smiled and brought her hand from behind her back, also showing two fingers. Shem started the fire beneath the caldron as Meshkel went to get two buckets of charcoal from the other fire pit. Once the sap was boiling, he stirred the charcoal into it. The mixture was still translucent, but now had a grayish tinge to it. He removed the caldron from the fire and poured two buckets full of the pitch. On the way to the ark, they stopped to pick up two brushes that were three-fingers wide, just perfect for the size of their buckets. They began at the bow of the keel beam and painted the three sides they could reach. When they ran out of pitch, they went back, and heated some more. They had used up that entire day's worth of pitch just before it was time for dinner. At supper they shared their day's adventure much to the smiles and congratulations of the rest of the family. One of the questions they asked Rayeh before they left the table was, "How many buckets of sap can we safely extract from each tree?" After they had prayed, Ham raised four fingers, as did his wife in confirmation. They all laughed, but before they turned in for the night, Shem and Meshkel went back to the trees, drilled holes, inserted straws, and set up buckets for a second batch that would be ready in the morning.

PART SIX
The Ark

Chapter Forty-Five
The Ark is Observed

The five kings of the north, Gareb, Nood, Raash, Dakak, and Alak all sat around Lucifer's table with his commanders, Haniel, Raziel and Balar. It was a council of war, although of a clandestine nature. When you rule a kingdom of rebellion and chaos, it tends to breed more of the same. He needed some kind of control, his nature demanded it, and these helped him to achieve it. The commander's armies were fiercely loyal. They had, after all, left heaven as a collective force. While confined to their human forms, they were still nearly invincible as a fighting force. The armies were as different as night and day and for that reason complimented each other completely.

Raziel and Balar ruled their armies with fear, intimidation, and pain. Haniel, on the other hand, commanded his armies with respect. There was nothing that his soldiers wouldn't do for him because they knew that he would do the same for them. He had proven it in battle time and time again. Each of the five kings had their own armies which they commanded and ruled with their new measure of power and authority. Together these held unquestioned dominion over the lands all around. The single exception were the lands of Noah.

Gareb stood, goblet in hand, a risky thing to do unbidden in Lucifer's presence. He raised the goblet, "My Lord Lucifer, to you and your unquestioned rule of our lands!" They each drank from their goblet, yet some warily, wondering what Gareb was up to. He continued, "My spies have discovered that Noah is building something to the north of the field of trees he planted so many years ago. We fear it may be some kind of weapon."

At Noah's name, Lucifer had turned and spat on the ground, but it was obvious that Gareb had piqued his interest. "Describe it to me."

"It is huge, my Lord, measuring three hundred cubits long and fifty cubits wide. It is built off the ground on logs, indicating that someday it may become mobile."

Now he definitely had Lucifer's attention, "And you think that it might be a weapon?"

Gareb smiled, "It's a little large for storing produce, my Lord."

Lucifer smiled at the joke too, "And why is this the first that I have heard of it?"

"With all due respect, my Lord, it is difficult to traverse through his forests," he added with his head bowed.

"But you were finally able to, where no others have been?" Lucifer questioned.

Gareb raised his head, "I have in my employ some of the best trackers, foresters, and spies in the kingdom."

Lucifer looked around the table, "and the rest of you?" They all hung their heads except Haniel.

Raash, one of the other kings, spoke, "Noah's forests are the stuff of legend. They are reported to be haunted and if the animals don't get you, it is said that the forest itself will devour you."

Lucifer smirked, "and you believe this tripe?"

Raash looked him squarely in the eye, which was unusual for any of them except Haniel. "I have lost too many men for me not to take the rumors seriously."

Lucifer looked directly at Haniel, "and you?"

"I worry more about the favor of Rayeh being with Noah than about any haunted forests or ravenous beasts."

Lucifer spat again, "You would use that name in my presence?" He was angry, agitated, perhaps even a tad bit afraid.

Haniel kept looking at him, straight in his eyes, "You asked, my Lord."

Lucifer took a deep calming breath. He must not look weak in front of his minions. Still speaking to Haniel, "Would you go check it out for me? I believe that you are related, are you not?"

"Yes, I am acquainted with Noah and his people. I will go and check out this building project." Haniel smiled. He liked having Lucifer over a barrel.

Haniel stood before his two most trusted commanders of one hundred, Jubiel and Zadok, "I have a rather delicate task to ask of you both. You have heard of Noah?"

Zadok looked to the ground, "It is rumored that the favor of Rayeh rests upon him and his house."

Haniel responded, "Zadok, look at me. You need never be afraid to answer me honestly and truthfully."

Zadok raised his head, "Yes, sir."

"We are going to pay him a visit," Haniel said matter-of-factly.

"My lord, it is said that uninvited that is not possible."

"Well, you may not know, but I am distantly related. I think he will see me. We will leave first thing in the morning." Haniel smiled, although if truth be told, he was a little apprehensive about meeting Noah face to face.

Chapter Forty-Six
Face to Face

They rode lightly, but warily up the road that led into Noah's land, their hands on the hilts of their swords. The road ran directly into the legendary haunted forest. Haniel stopped, dismounted, and his men quickly followed suit. Out of the forest stepped an eight-cubit tall angel, wings and all. Haniel removed his sword, took a knee, and placed his sword on the ground with both hands.

Haniel kept his head bowed, "Lord R'gal, it has been a long time."

When R'gal spoke, the very air about them echoed with the authority of his words. "You do not need to address me as lord. I am but an angel as are you, albeit unfallen. What brings you here?"

"Lucifer has learned of Noah's building project and has dispatched me to find out more about it." Haniel looked up, "May I stand?"

R'gal became a man, different than the one Haniel was used to, but there was still something regal about his bearing. "Certainly, and thank you for the respect. We did not part on particularly friendly terms."

Haniel stood, "True, but I will always respect you." He paused, "If it is possible, I would like to speak with Noah about his project."

"Do you mind leaving your sword and your two men here?" R'gal asked.

"No, that is fine. May I ride?" He gestured to the horse.

"Yes," and a majestic bay mare stepped out of the forest and walked up next to R'gal. "While you are here, please address me as Regem."

Haniel's stallion was visibly disturbed by Regem's elegant mare. "Is Regem another one of your famous disguises?" he chuckled.

Regem just shrugged his shoulders, but smiled himself, and mounted the mare.

They rode side-by-side up the road towards Noah's.

"Did you know that they say these forests are haunted?" Haniel now smiled.

"Protected might be more accurate." Regem continued his faint smile too.

"That's how I would have put it if asked, but I wasn't asked."

"How is Lucifer?" His voice might have contained a note of sincere concern.

"About the same," Haniel chuckled, "I mentioned Rayeh's name and he noticeably cringed, and spat on the ground. I'm sure he knows that his days are numbered. That's why Noah's building project has him so worried."

Regem looked intently at Haniel, "What does he think that it is?"

"Some say that because it is off the ground and resting on logs that it may be some kind of movable weapon." Haniel looked off into the forest.

"A three hundred cubit long movable weapon? What are we going to do, fill it with an army and drive it up to the city gates?" Regem shook his head in disbelief. "Who said that, one of his puppet kings?"

"That was Gareb, not the brightest star in the heavens."

"And what do you think?" Regem asked pointedly.

Haniel took a deep breath, "I'm afraid you are not going to be able to tell me and Lucifer won't like that at all when I go back to report."

"Well, I can tell you this much, it is not a weapon." He had cleared that remark with Rayeh earlier.

They left the horses with a stable hand and walked up to the house. The first thing that surprised Haniel was that there was no guard at the door. Regem took him all the way through the house to the sitting room, where there were actually chairs instead of cushions, another surprise. Regem sat in one and gestured to another. Haniel also sat to another surprise. The chairs were very comfortable indeed and you could use both hands simultaneously without having to rest on an elbow.

"This place is full of surprises." He paused a moment. "I'm not sure what I expected, but this exceeds it." He paused again, "luxury without opulence."

"You might also be surprised to find out that Noah designed and constructed all this furniture himself," Regem added proudly.

They were interrupted by Juniel, who entered with a tray of refreshments.

"Ah…Juniel, who brightens every room she enters," Regem almost sang to Juniel's blushing. He gestured towards Haniel, "May I present Haniel, one of the fallen."

Haniel blanched at the reference to his fallen state, but recovered quickly, "My pleasure to meet you, Juniel," he spoke to her downcast eyes. He was even on his way towards standing in her presence when Noah himself entered the room. Haniel was caught off guard and struggled to maintain his balance. It was obvious that Rayeh's favor did rest on Noah as almost a cloak of its own kind of regality. Haniel bowed, "Master Noah." He had some difficulty even getting the words out.

Regem had also stood, whether it was for Juniel's entrance or Noah's was hard to distinguish, "My lord, this is Haniel," and he gestured to his bowed form.

Noah smiled, "Ah yes, I recognize him."

Haniel wondered, *"How?"*

Regem winked at Juniel and she turned to leave, but Juniel stopped when Regem added, "Haniel is wondering about your building project. Lucifer is worried."

Noah spoke to Juniel's back, "It's okay, Juniel. We live under the protection of Rayeh." Juniel visibly relaxed and continued out of the room. Noah had expected Haniel to flinch at Rayeh's name, but he had not. "Please be seated," he spoke to the men. He looked to Regem, "What have you told him?"

Regem looked non-plussed, "Only that it isn't a weapon."

Noah chuckled at that, "That would have been a little cumbersome, a three-hundred-cubit long weapon. It would take an army just to move it, let alone wield it as a weapon."

Haniel too smiled, "My thoughts exactly, but you know Lucifer."

Noah looked to Regem, "I have heard stories. Well, now that I have confirmed that it is not a weapon," Noah had stepped to the table and filled the cups with wine, "What else would you like to know?" He handed Haniel a cup, then Regem.

"Can you tell me anything else about your project?" Haniel almost pleaded.

Noah looked at Regem, who nodded, "I do not wish to offend you, but if I may speak plainly?"

Haniel took a long drink and sat forward in his chair, "It is your house, sir."

Noah began, "The entire world is enveloped in chaos. Evil grows more evil by the day, so much so that Rayeh has decided to end it all!"

Haniel seemed confused, "End it all?"

"He is going to destroy everything in which is the breath of life, everything except that which we can save with the project." Noah took a long drink. Haniel still didn't understand. Noah continued, "Sometimes when we go on a picnic to the river that borders our land, we float the empty picnic basket in the river, and run along the bank until we can catch it." Haniel seemed to get that picture. "Rayeh is going to flood the earth with so much water that it will cover all of the land and all in whom is the breath of life will die except that which I save in the large basket I am building."

Haniel seemed to ponder it, "Where will all that water come from?"

"It will fall from the sky and burst forth from the earth. He assures me there is enough water."

"And only those who are in the basket will be saved?" Although it was incredible, it seemed to make sense. Haniel became a little cynical, "And how will you decide who to save?"

Noah took a long deep breath, "I won't have to decide. Other than my family and the animals we will collect? No one else will repent of their evil, believe the flood will happen, and ask to join us."

Haniel studied the floor, "No one else will ask?" Then he slowly looked up.

Noah reached out his hand, "Would you like to join us?" His sincere compassion brought tears to Regem's eyes.

Haniel's eyes joined Noah's, "I'm afraid that I crossed a line at the death of my son from which there is no return," and he stood. "Thanks for the wine. I can see myself out."

Regem stood anyway, "I will walk you to the stables." It was a statement of fact, not a question.

At the stables Haniel mounted his horse. Regem reached up and placed his hand on the horse's neck, "You could come with us." His voice also rang with sincere compassion.

Haniel smiled weakly, "You probably need to talk to your friend, Rayeh, about that," and he patted Regem's hand, "but thanks for the offer." He stood a little straighter in the saddle. "Now how am I going to explain that to Lucifer?" and he spurred his horse into a trot.

Chapter Forty-Seven
Lucifer's Response

The council of war met again in Lucifer's chambers. They all sat stunned, except Haniel who had just reported Noah's words to Lucifer. Lucifer was furious beyond words. When he finally gathered himself enough to speak, his voice dripped with venom, "This is an act of war! We will destroy him and his 'basket'!" The way he sneered the word 'basket' made it painful to listen to.

Haniel's words were measured, "You would wage war against heaven again?"

Lucifer, still enraged, turned and tried to slap him, but Haniel caught Lucifer's hand. He held it for a moment as he also held his gaze, then he let Lucifer's hand slowly loose.

"I suggest that you never raise your hand against me again," Haniel calmly confronted him.

Lucifer spat out, "Gather your armies! I want you to be the first to assault him!"

Haniel turned and began walking away. He uttered over his shoulder, "No! Any war against heaven is foolish and futile!" and left Lucifer's chambers.

Lucifer shouted after him, "You will disobey my orders?" but Haniel was already gone. He yelled behind the retreating form he could no longer see, "You will regret this!" The rest of the table looked sideways at one another. They were afraid to speak. Lucifer took a deep breath, then another. Then he said rather calmly, "Raziel?"

Raziel tried to respond with his normal military precision, but was still reeling from the spectacle. "My Lord," he squeaked out.

"Will you gather your army and seek to engage Noah and destroy his basket for me?" His words were measured.

"Yes, my Lord." He paused. "Now, my Lord?"

Lucifer looked at him menacingly, "Sooner would be much better than later. Yes, now!"

Raziel stood, "Of course, my Lord!" and left the chambers.

Lucifer looked slowly around the table, "Ensure that your armies are also ready to move upon my call Balar, especially yours. Dismissed!" Lucifer turned the other way and retreated towards his throne room.

Haniel stood before commander Zadok, "I have a request to make of you. It is not an order."

Zadok's arm still crossed his chest where he had just made his salute, "You have but to ask, my lord."

Haniel stepped to the table before them, poured a goblet of chilled wine and set it on the table. He gestured for Zadok to recline at the table and did so himself. "As you know, my relationship with Lord Lucifer," and he lifted his eyebrows at the word 'lord', "is tenuous at best." He studied Zadok's reaction, "He has asked me to lead a war against Noah and I have declined."

"Is that wise, my lord?" Zadok questioned.

"We lost one fight against heaven. I am not about to engage in another. I told him as much." Haniel still watched

Zadok closely. While he trusted him, he needed to be sure of his complete allegiance. Divided loyalties at this point would not suffice with what he planned. He continued, "Lucifer had the audacity to try and slap me in front of his war council." Haniel smiled. "He was unsuccessful and I doubt he will try anything that overt again."

"And…?" Zadok asked.

"I walked out on him. He will have to engage this war without my help, but we must move quickly." He took another drink. "I want you to carry a message to Noah that Lucifer plans to attack him."

Zadok took his own large drink of wine, "Now, sir?"

"Yes, immediately." Zadok set down his cup and began to stand. "I believe that if you follow the same route we last took that you will undoubtedly be met by the archangel R'gal again."

"May I give him the message or must I give it to Noah personally?"

"We will let R'gal determine that." Haniel also stood. He reached out to clasp Zadok's forearm, pulled him into an embrace, and whispered in his ear, "Thank you."

When they stepped back, Zadok's eyes glistened, "Anything for you, my lord!" and Haniel knew that it was more than just words.

Haniel was correct, as Zadok approached the forest on the road to Noah's, Regem trotted out on his majestic bay mare. Zadok's stallion stopped as though struck, obviously smitten, almost throwing Zadok over his head. Zadok reached down and patted his neck. The horse breathed huskily. Zadok dismounted, as did Regem.

Regem smiled mischievously, "To what pleasure do I owe this visit?"

Zadok couldn't help but ask, "How do you always know when we are coming?"

Regem continued to smile, "Trade secret, sorry. How can I help? Zadok, isn't it?"

"Actually, I have come to help you. Haniel sent me to warn you that Lucifer has declared war on Noah."

"Really, why would he want to do that?" Regem seemed surprised.

"Lucifer or Haniel?" Zadok was unsure of the question.

"Both."

"Well, Haniel shared with Lucifer what Noah had told him about the flood and your basket," he began.

"That would have been interesting to hear," chuckled Regem.

"Lucifer was furious and wanted to send Haniel to attack you at once, but Haniel would have nothing to do with it. He said, 'One war with heaven was enough.' Lucifer even tried to slap Haniel for saying it, but was unable to connect. Haniel turned his back on Lucifer's council of war and left." Zadok shared it all in one long breath then stopped to inhale deeply. "Then he sent me here to warn you."

"And thank you and him for doing that! What will Haniel do now?" R'gal was concerned for Haniel's safety. Lucifer was not easily spurned.

"Lucifer is not foolish enough to try and start a war with us too, especially if he's going to go ahead with his war on you. Haniel will be careful, but Lucifer has just alienated a third of his angelic army." Zadok met Regem's eyes, "What will you do?"

Regem looked off to the right. "You know they say these forests are haunted. It's more that they are protected. As unlikely as it may seem, we can take care of ourselves, but again thank him for the warning." He reached up into his saddlebag and retrieved something wrapped in a silk kerchief, "Could you give him this for me? A gift from a friend." He reached it out to Zadok.

"What is it?" Zadok was curious. It was as large as his fist and as heavy as a stone.

"There is a note inside explaining it." Regem reached out his hand again and Zadok grasped his forearm, "and Zadok, you are always welcome here." With that Regem turned and mounted the mare. She whinnied and Zadok's stallion shook his head in response. Regem added, "I will pass on the information to Noah, but I can assure you of his thanks too." He trotted back up the road towards Noah's.

Zadok put the parcel in his own saddlebag and mounted his stallion, who seemed reluctant to leave the departing mare and her rider, and turned him back towards the way he had come. When he arrived at Haniel's, he dropped off his stallion at the stable, removed the parcel from his saddlebag, and walked to Haniel's home. Known to Haniel's guards, Zadok was ushered into the home and into the care of one of the servants who took him to the sitting room, where a table was prepared with wine and other refreshments. Haniel's servant assured him that the master would be with him shortly. Zadok took a goblet of wine, but decided to await his lord standing rather than reclining at the table. He still held the parcel in his other hand, almost reluctant to let it go. He only had to wait a moment for Haniel to arrive.

"Zadok, I trust things went well?" and Haniel approached with an outstretched arm. Zadok had set his goblet down and now firmly grasped his lord's arm.

"Yes, my lord. It went well. In fact, Regem asked me to give you this gift, a token of his and Noah's thanks for your warning." He extended the parcel to him.

Haniel took it, surprised at its weight, and motioned for Zadok to take his place at the table. Haniel knelt at the table and unwrapped the parcel. It was a translucent blue stone, as large as his fist. He spread out on the table the note that had accompanied it, and read it aloud. "This is one of the Zedekeem, the stones of Rightness. It will allow us to speak to one another regardless of the distance that lies between us. Take it in both hands, look into it, and call my name." Haniel looked at Zadok, "I have heard of these, but I have never seen one. Shall we try it?" Zadok nodded, albeit a little reluctantly. Haniel had never seen Zadok afraid and wondered if this was what he looked like when he feared something or someone.

Haniel picked up the stone in both hands and called out, "Regem?" The stone seemed to brighten and Regem's face appeared in the stone. Haniel almost dropped it.

"Ah, you have received our gift." It was a statement of fact. "You can reach me or Noah at any time with it," another fact. "Place it somewhere very safe as it is of immeasurable value."

"Do you have a stone too?" Haniel questioned.

Regem smiled, "No, we can access your stone without the need for another stone on our end. You, or someone you trust, will need to be within hearing distance of your stone though for it to work for you."

Haniel's eyes were filled with wonder and he muttered, "Thank you, this is a gift beyond measure."

Regem responded immediately, "And thank you for the warning of Lucifer's intentions. Do not let anyone else, especially Lucifer, know that you possess one of these stones. Although he would not be able to operate it, he would think that he could, and would stop at nothing to possess one."

Now Haniel wondered if he should be afraid of the stone.

"Use it only in time of need, as Lucifer may be able to sense that it exists in his realm. Until next time," and the stone darkened as Regem's face disappeared.

Chapter Forty-Eight
An Unusual War

Days later when Haniel received word that Lucifer had implemented his planned attack of Noah's realm he took the stone of Rightness in his hands again, "Regem?" Regem's face appeared in the stone. "Lucifer has dispatched Raziel and his army to attack you."

Regem seemed pleased to receive the news, "Thank you for the warning. You need not be anxious; we are prepared to receive them." The stone darkened.

Raziel, with six of his commanders flanking him in a semi-circle, stood on horseback before the road that entered Noah's haunted forest. Noah on his white stallion and Regem on his bay mare, rode out of the forest and stood with the blazing morning sun at their back.

Regem looked over his shoulder towards the sun, "I think I have you at a disadvantage." He was even faintly smiling.

Raziel laughed derisively, "The two of you against my vast hoard? That is preposterous!"

Regem spoke, still faintly smiling, "You only see the two of us. There are more here for us than there are of you against us. Perhaps a small demonstration would help? Send forth your most fearsome commander."

Raziel looked to his right hand and Koor and his stallion stepped forth.

Regem addressed him, "You are one of the fallen, Noah is just a man," and he looked at Noah.

Rayeh whispered to Noah's heart, *"You may dismount."*

Noah dismounted and took a few steps towards Koor. "You will notice Noah is unarmed."

Noah slowly lifted his hands up and away from his sides to show that he was indeed unarmed. Koor drew his sword, a sly smile making its way across his face. He even licked his lips in anticipation of what was coming.

Rayeh whispered again, *"Bring down your right hand."* Noah made a downward gesture with his right hand and the sword fell from Koor's hand. Koor's eyes widened in surprise. *"Now, your left."* Noah gestured down with his left hand and Koor stiffened and fell off his horse, fortunately on his shoulder, or he might have broken his neck.

Regem addressed Raziel, "Who would like to be next?"

Tudar, the commander to Raziel's left, urged his stallion confidently forward.

Rayeh whispered, *"Raise and lower both hands."* As Tudar's hand went to the hilt of his sword, Noah quickly raised and lowered both his hands and Tudar stiffened and fell off his horse to join Koor.

Regem addressed Raziel a final time. "I suggest your other commanders pick up Koor and Tudar, lash them across their horses, and that you all leave while you still can."

Before Raziel could even speak a word, the other commanders scrambled off their horses to comply, grabbed the two commanders off the ground, lashed them to their horses, and remounted. The rest of Raziel's army had already turned tail and were retreating at a full gallop. Raziel stood alone on his horse before Noah and Regem, petrified.

Noah spoke for the first time and his words glistened with power, "Tell your prince that neither he nor you are welcomed on my land, ever!" Raziel turned his horse around and walked dejectedly back the way he had come.

Noah remounted his white stallion and he and Regem turned back towards home. "I'd hate to have to be the one that gets to report that confrontation to Lucifer," and they both laughed.

However, they failed to notice one horseman cloaked all in black, near the tree line, who had not retreated with the others. He dismounted, then pulled a bow and quiver from a bag tied to his horse. He slung the quiver over his shoulder, strung the bow, and stepped into the trees. Lucifer walked silently about fifty cubits into the forest and sat on a stump. This was going to prove more difficult than he had envisioned. He nocked an arrow, listened silently, and waited. A rabbit hopped into view a short distance away. He drew bead, released his arrow and watched it skewer the rabbit. He lay his bow on the stump and walked to where the rabbit thrashed in circles. He picked it up, withdrew his arrow, and choked the rabbit to death. Back at the stump, he grabbed a handful of grass and wiped his arrow and knife clean before replacing them in the quiver and sheath. He lay his bow on the grass, disemboweled the rabbit on the stump, and ate its liver and heart raw. He skinned the rabbit, lay it fur side up on the bloody stump, sat on it and proceeded to think. *"Hmmm, what should my next move be against Noah?"* he mused. He continued thinking to himself, *"There must be some way to enter this forest unseen. I have ventured this far, hmmm."* He almost asked aloud, *"And who is it that rides with Noah on the bay?"*

Lucifer sat on his throne. It was ornate beyond opulence. Raziel knelt before him, his head bowed, his sword on the floor before him, "I have failed you, my Lord."

Lucifer's words cut to the quick, "You did not just fail, you were humiliated by a human. If you had lost to an archangel I might understand, but to an unarmed man using parlor tricks?"

Raziel ventured, "They were more than just parlor…"

"SILENCE!" Lucifer screamed. "I did not give you permission to speak!"

Raziel flinched, wondering who had betrayed him. He had come almost straight to the throne room to report, although he had to admit he was in no hurry to tell Lucifer of his failure.

"Here is what you are going to do," Lucifer sneered. "Every day, one of your men will seek to penetrate further and further into Noah's forest, until we have broken the hold of the," and he laughed outright, "haunted forest." He continued, "Begin with those two fools who fell off their horses."

Raziel submissively answered, "Yes, sir."

He might have said more, but Lucifer cut him off, "Dismissed, get out of my sight! If he had been half the angel he should have been, he would have grabbed his sword and removed Lucifer's ugly head, but in-stead he got slowly up, and backed out of Lucifer's presence, his head still bowed.

If he had been half the angel he should have been, he would have grabbed his sword and removed Lucifer's ugly head, but instead he got slowly up, removed his sword, laid it at his feet, backed out of Lucifer's presence, his head still bowed. As he walked out the large paneled doors of Lucifer's throne room, he nearly bumped into his two commanders, the fools who fell off their horses, Koor and Tudar.

Before he could say anything to them, he heard Lucifer bellow, "Koor, Tudar, come before me!" They reluctantly entered Lucifer's presence, shaking in their boots. Raziel hoped they would leave with their heads still attached to their bodies. The door slammed behind them and Raziel slowly made the trek, step by step, back to the stables for his horse.

Reclined at his table, Raziel contemplated getting rip roaring drunk, which was difficult for an angel, even a fallen one. Koor and Tudar walked slowly in unannounced, like two dogs with their tails between their legs.

"Well, you still have your heads," Raziel muttered.

"Lucifer had sincerely considered having us flogged," Tudar shared.

Raziel stood slowly, filled them each a flagon of wine, and handed it to them saying, "Now, let's figure out what we must do to get back in our Lord's good graces."

"That's simple," remarked Koor, "destroy Noah and the weapon he is building."

"Haniel said it wasn't a weapon," retorted Raziel.

Tudar responded, "He probably lied."

Chapter Forty-Nine
Before a Haunted Forest

Lucifer gave them directions to the spot where he had entered the forest without telling them how he knew it existed. It increased his mystique, gave the appearance of a plan, and made it seem he still had a measure of control. The plan, while simple, proved not to be easy. They had anticipated that much. They were to cut a new road through the forest to Noah's and do it stealthily. The forest cooperated on no level at all. They kept meeting wild beasts which attacked and quickly dispatched the non-angelic. Even the forest itself seemed to fight against them. They would attempt to fall a tree and it would cause more problems than it solved. Clearing up the debris afterwards became much more difficult after the tree had fallen. After a full year they had made hardly any progress at all.

At the end of the same year, Noah, his family, and Regem sat around Noah's dinner table. The evening meal concluded, Juniel had just removed the dishes, and Regem had just finished telling them a funny story. As the laughter subsided, he added, "On a more somber note. This is the first anniversary of our beginning to build the ark. I have calculated, from our progress, that it should only take us about one hundred years to complete it.

Shem looked around the table and laughed, "Another joke?"

Regem shook his head, "No, I'm being quite serious."

Ham, "One hundred years? You are sure of your calculations?"

Regem nodded, "I rechecked them a number of times."

"Is there any way we can shorten that time?" Noah asked.

Regem sighed, "I don't think so. The process is a pretty efficient use of our limited manpower." He looked around, "No offense ladies. I doubt that anyone will help us. The word has spread to the surrounding villages, towns, even the cities concerning Noah and his silly large basket. They don't want any part of our foolishness. They mostly mock us."

Naamah added, "From their perspective, I imagine it does look pretty silly. Water is going to fall from the sky? Why not vegetables?"

Japheth asked, "What about Lucifer's road through the forest?"

Regem replied, "That will take him almost as long and he's not known for his patience. I'm sure he will take some more overt action, soon."

Lucifer, mounted on his great gray stallion, stood surrounded by over one hundred archers as Noah and Regem rode out of the forest on the road that led to their home. Lucifer raised his hand and all the archers drew their bows. He loudly commanded, "Noah, get down off that horse."

Noah smiled, rested his hands in his lap and responded to him without even addressing him by name. "You have no authority here!"

Lucifer cut his hand down sharply and at that precise moment every archer's bowstring snapped. Arrows fell to the ground and clattered onto the road. Lucifer looked all around him.

"Didn't Raziel tell you what happened when he confronted me?" Noah spoke with his own voice of command. Lucifer reached for his dark sword as Noah heard a familiar whisper and swiftly raised his hand. Lucifer's horse reared, nearly dislodging him. Noah brought his hand back down, the horse came back down with it, again jolting Lucifer.

"Lower both hands." Noah lowered both his hand towards the ground and Lucifer's horse knelt before him. "See, your horse has more sense than you." Lucifer pulled back madly at the reigns, but to no avail.

Lucifer called out, "You will regret this!"

Noah spoke slowly, yet powerfully the words he was hearing. "Judgment is coming, the end of all things in which there is the breath of life. The time is at hand. The world will be covered in water, so deeply that there will no longer be any land. All will drown, except those who accompany me on the ark, the basket," Noah chuckled at the word "basket," "that I am building." He continued again seriously, "There is room for you to come. If you repent of your evil, your rebellion against Rayeh, and choose to come with us, you may come. I plead with you to come with us. Come now!"

Noah folded his hands in front of him and Lucifer's horse struggled to its feet.

Lucifer laughed, "You fool, where is all this water? It will not come. My subjects are safe with me. It is you who will be destroyed and I will see to it!" He sneered, grasped his dark sword, and pulled it from its scabbard. At the same time

Noah heard a whisper and slowly raised his hand. When Noah's hand reached its peak, Lucifer's sword, fully raised, fell from his hand and clattered to the ground.

Noah walked over to the sword as Lucifer screamed, "Do not touch it!"

Noah stopped for a moment as if listening, because he was. Then he stooped and picked up the sword by its hilt. No one had ever held the sword unless Lucifer had handed it to them. He shuddered in his saddle. Noah inspected the sword, marveling at its workmanship. It was, after all, one of the eight swords Alathos had forged before time began. Noah stepped next to Lucifer's horse. It should have shied away from the blade, but stood transfixed. Normally when handing someone a blade, you handed it to them hilt first. Noah did not. He raised the sword to Lucifer and made him grasp it by the blade. In doing so, Lucifer sliced his hand.

He winced in pain, blood dripping from the wound. "You fool," he said again, and tried to turn the horse away, but it still stood as if frozen to the spot.

Noah spoke quietly so that only Lucifer could hear him. "I do not mean to ridicule or embarrass you. You were at one time the prince of the seven, but you chose to leave that estate and no longer rule where I stand." Lucifer visibly recoiled in shock. Noah continued, "I have not given you leave to be excused from my presence nor the presence of the Creator of the Universe." Lucifer blanched. Noah turned his back on him and spoke over his shoulder, "Now, you may go." Noah mounted his stallion and he and Regem turned to ride back up the road to his home.

Lucifer remained there speechless until they were gone. He asked himself again, "*Who is it that rides with Noah?*" Then he turned his horse around and headed back to his palace. His army just stood there. He had given them no order. Finally, Raziel spoke, "Back to the palace!" and their ranks haphazardly turned around to straggle after Lucifer in disarray.

That was the last direct confrontation between Lucifer and Noah until the day the rains fell, although Lucifer continued to try and build his "not so secret" road through the haunted forest. That process continued to move slowly, fraught with peril.

Chapter Fifty
The Building Continues

Noah and his family went back to the process of building the ark with renewed vigor. It was a significant comfort to hear the story of Lucifer's debacle and the obvious protection and favor that they lived under. Their singing as they worked modulated from light hearted to joyfully boisterous.

As the years passed, the ark began to take shape. When they celebrated a quarter of a century's worth of work, they had the entire length of the hull built up to one-third its height. When they had the lower floor and the first deck installed, it was a joyous occasion. However, there were some events that were momentous for a different reason. Enoch's wife, Japhia, died at nearly five hundred years of age. She got to see four generations of her family grow and mature and even witnessed much of the early building of the ark, from the planting of Noah and Naamah's seedlings, to the harvesting of those same trees to make lumber for the ark. She was a wonderful woman and passed away in her great great granddaughter's arms one evening under the stars.

Japhia's passing was difficult, even while they were all assured that she was with Rayeh. However, the most difficult passing for Regem was Juniel's. As Noah's servant and Regem's friend she had lived to a ripe old age and they had many wonderful memories together. The one Regem would always recall most fondly began one night, near the fire pit under the stars. They had shared many such nights, but this one was uniquely special.

"I have told you of the times I became a horse?"

Juniel nodded bashfully.

"I would like to try something different tonight, close your eyes."

She did. "No peeking," and she winked her still closed eye.

"Okay, you can open them," and there before her stood, not the elegant black stallion of before, but a majestic one that was also a centaur. He smiled, "Even I wasn't sure I could pull this off." His smile deepened, "Would you like to ride?" She nodded.

He reached down, grasped her by the forearm, and gracefully swung her onto his back. He reached both his hands behind him, "Give me your hands." He pulled her hands forwards, crisscrossed them around his chest, then pulled her close to his back. "Hold on tight." He was smiling broadly, so was she, as she laid her head on his shoulder, her hair cascading over it.

She lifted her head, whispered in his ear, "What is love?"

He had just begun to walk and was so startled that he stumbled. She instantly held him tighter. Hmm, he liked that. Maybe he should stumble more often, but he responded, "You're sure you want to start this ride with that question?" He wondered if he were blushing.

"Yes?" and she left it open for him to begin.

"Well, let's see, there are different types or kinds of love. There is fondness, friendship, family love, infatuation, passion, and what I might call, for lack of a better term, unselfish love."

She spoke rather breathlessly in his ear, "and do you love me?" There, she had asked him.

"Yes," he chuckled, "I am a little fond of you, in a friendly sort of way.""

She let go of him with her right arm and slapped him on the flank, "You know what I mean."

"Do I," and he reached back and patted her on the thigh, "maybe you need to explain your question."

Although he couldn't see her blush, he could feel the heat radiating from her. "You once said we could never be more than friends. Is that still true?"

Regem threw a quick plea up to Rayeh for help. "You're asking if we can be more than friends?"

"Yes," she whispered.

He was treading carefully now, "We are both part of Noah's family, so I think we have progressed that far. I would say that I love you unselfishly too."

"And passionately?" she queried.

"There are also different levels and kinds of passion. When a man and a woman are called 'lovers' it usually means that they have become physically intimate. That kind of love is forbidden between angels and women," he added sadly.

She picked up on his sadness. "Are you sad because that kind of love is forbidden to you and I?"

Wow, she was asking the difficult questions tonight. "Yes, that, and because I saw the consequences of crossing that line. The cost was catastrophic. While Lucifer lost his place in heaven due to misplaced pride and many of the other fallen lost theirs because of misplaced loyalty, there were also the consequences to having intimate relations with women, the Ashereem. I don't want us to make the same mistake."

"You mean it is possible for us to have children?" She wasn't making this any easier.

"Of the over forty that tried to conceive, only twenty lived to maturity." He hoped that would stop the conversation. They continued to ride along in silence.

She finally whispered, "Thank you for your honesty. I don't want to have children with you. I already love you as much as I can and believe you love me as much as you are allowed," and she held him tightly for a long time, until he feared to take too deep a breath and break the moment. She whispered slyly, "You should sing me a song," and laughed.

"Wait a minute, I'm doing all the work here!" he chortled.

"Yes," she added, "isn't it grand?" She broke into a tender love song of a lonely hunter and the white doe he often spied near a crystal-clear mountain lake. When she finished the song, they were back where they started. He offered her an arm and she slid off his back. In an instant he was a man again and she hadn't even closed her eyes. He offered her his hand and she took it. They walked back slowly to the fire. He lay down, she lay cradled in his arms, and they watched the stars circle in their silent courses above. The fire had died when they finally got up and went back into the house.

The night of her passing, they were also by the fire pit, watching the stars move slowly in the sky. She had fallen asleep in his arms when she breathed her last breath and Rayeh himself stepped through a portal.

"It's time," he said in his most compassionate voice. Rayeh reached out and touched her hand. Her eyes fluttered open and he helped her to her feet. She was a radiant young woman again, in the prime of her life.

She looked back lovingly at Regem, "Goodbye, my love."

He blew her a kiss, "No, this is not goodbye. We will never have to say goodbye. I will see you 'soon.'" *"Soon,"* he thought to himself, *"such an interesting, but non-exact word."* She gave Rayeh a hug and hand in hand they walked back through the portal.

Chapter Fifty-One
It is Time

Haniel held the stone in his hands, "Regem?"

"Yes, I am here."

Haniel whispered, "Lucifer and all of his forces are gathering for an assault on you and your ark. He has completed his secret road through your forest."

"Thank you, Haniel. We have always known of his attempt to build a road through our forest and we are prepared." Regem spoke in a whisper too, just in case Haniel was in a place where he didn't want to be overheard. "You need to say goodbye to any human friends or animals that you care about, for the end of all flesh is at hand." His words were solemn and grave.

There was a hesitation, then, "Thank you, I will do that." Another pause, "And Regem," surprisingly he added, "the favor of Rayeh go with you," and the stone darkened.

It had taken them nearly the entire week, but finally the ark was complete, the provisions were aboard. It was almost difficult to believe, that after all these years, what Rayeh had spoken so long ago would soon be fulfilled. Regem had said that animals would begin arriving in the morning. Noah and his family had one final night in the old world. Sleep for most of them came fitfully, except for Regem and the angelic shepherds. They spent the night gathering the nocturnal animals for the procession in the morning.

The dark and evil world still dawned beautifully on Noah's land, the one place on the planet where they held darkness at bay. The family gathered on both sides of the pathway that led from the forest to the boarding ramp of the ark. The men lined one side and the women the other side. Initially the ramp was attached to the upper deck floor of the ark where the smaller animals would be welcomed. At its top stood Regem and the angel Uriel to point the animals towards their designated domain. At the end of the family line and about halfway to the forest stood the angels Michael and Raphael. The family had just recently met them and were still a little in awe of them, even though they were in their human form. Somewhere in the forest Gabriel directed traffic.

A lion roared, sounding like the king of beasts that he was. Regem followed with, "It begins!" Meshkel and Mashal started the song they had composed for the animal procession and out of the forest marched a line of small common animals in pairs: mice, moles, rats, and weasels. They were followed by rabbits, raccoons, cats and dogs. Pairs of birds also accompanied them: ravens, owls, hawks, pelicans, and eagles. This continued until it was time for the intermediate-sized animals and the ramp was repositioned to the second level. Now came the jaguars, lions, horses, even two apes and two monkeys. Then they were followed by animals in pairs of seven, because they were special and not common. They were sheep, goats, deer, antelope and of the birds: doves, pigeons, turkeys, ducks, and geese. This continued until the intermediate deck was filled and they moved the ramp to the lower deck. Then came the pairs of large common animals: two camels, two hippos, two rhinos, two elephants. They were followed by the large special animals; seven pairs of buffalo, oxen, cows, until all the animals were aboard.

As the sun set, Noah and his family climbed the ramp. His family entered the ark and proceeded to their quarters, leaving Noah and Regem alone on the ramp. Regem pointed out to Noah, "Lucifer's two armies!"

Down Lucifer's supposedly secret road on the right and Noah's road on the left poured two armies of Lucifer's to assemble before the ark. A line of archers interspersed with horsemen carrying torches, stood in front with a line of foot soldiers behind them. Noah and Regem simply waited until their ranks were fully formed.

Lucifer rode forward to shout, "Disembark or I will destroy this abomination."

Noah took one step down the ramp towards Lucifer. "This is not your domain; I forbid you to speak!"

Lucifer tried to speak again, but found that he could not. He began to turn purple with anger, waving his arms and frantically gesturing.

Noah continued, "The end of all flesh is at hand. Water will fall from the skies for forty days and forty nights. The fountains of the deep will open to spew forth water and all the earth will be covered in a flood. All in whom is the breath of life will perish, except those who accompany me on the ark. This is your last chance to join us, come!"

A soldier broke through the ranks, dropping his sword, "I will come!" An arrow pierced him back to front, clean through, and he fell dead to the ground.

"Who loosed that arrow?" commanded Raziel. His commander, Tudar, raised his empty bow. Raziel laughed in derision, "Any others care to join that soldier?" he sneered.

Regem stepped to Noah's side and whispered, "He was a spy." Noah turned and strode up the ramp and into the ark as Regem strode down to the ground. Regem stepped to one side of the ramp and turned into all of his eight-cubit glory.

Lucifer was aghast, "R'gal? I slew you in the rebellion!" He choked on the revelation.

Someone else stepped out of the darkness to the other side. Together they removed the ramp and pushed the large door into place.

Lucifer found his voice, "Add fire to the arrows!" The archers lit their arrows off the torches. "Ready!" They pulled them back, prepared to release them. R'gal turned around and the increased light of the arrows revealed the other man to be Rayeh.

"Fire!" yelled Lucifer as a portal opened, R'gal and Rayeh stepped through it, and the heavens opened to release a deluge of rain. The arrows were quenched and driven to the ground short of their mark. "NO!" screamed Lucifer, who was soon drenched to the bone. It had begun!

Chapter Fifty-Two
After the Flood

The sound of the rain on the roof, while initially startling, soon became soothing, its steady rhythm resounding through the ark. All the animals and birds rested in their assigned places and many of them began to fall asleep. Then the ship moved. The entire ship moved. The water outside the ship had reached a level that lifted the ship off the timbers on which it had rested. The rocking of the ship coupled with the rhythm of the rain put everyone in the ark to sleep except the birds. The birds remained contented to sit on their perches and eat out of the boxes of seed provided for them.

And it rained as Noah had said, for forty days and forty nights. Then Rayeh restrained the heavens from raining and closed up the fountains of the deep. When the rain stopped, Rayeh also sent a wind over all the earth to begin to dry it. At the end of one hundred and fifty days the waters had abated enough so that the ark came to rest on the mountains of Ararat. For two and a half more months the waters continued to dry up. At the end of forty days Noah opened the window that he had made in the ark and released a raven to see if the waters had receded enough. Then he sent forth a dove which returned to the ark having found no place on which to set her foot. After seven more days, he released her again and this time she returned with a freshly plucked olive branch in her beak and Noah knew that the waters had receded and life was beginning to appear again. He waited one more week and released the dove again. This time she did not return.

Noah opened the hatch of the ark, looked out, and sure enough all the water had receded. The ground had appeared and it was dry, yet it was another fifty-seven days before Rayeh opened the door of the ark and said, "Come out Noah, you and your wife, your sons and their wives. Bring with you every living thing in which is the breath of life which we have rescued: all the birds, animals, and everything that creeps upon the earth. Let them be fruitful, multiply, and cover the face of the earth."

Then they all left the ark, Noah and his family, and every bird, beast, and creeping thing by their families.

All the animals stood around as Noah and his sons built an altar from the unhewn stones nearby. Then Noah spoke to the animals, "Who among you would give his life as a sacrifice of thanksgiving for the Lord's deliverance of our lives through the flood?" Of every special beast and bird, one of their males stepped forward and formed a line to the altar, to be slain, and burnt on it as a thanksgiving sacrifice.

As the line came to an end, there stood Rayeh, tears coursing down his cheeks, "Never again will I curse the ground because of man. Never again will I strike down everything within whom is the breath of life as I have just done. While the earth remains, there will be day and night, hot and cold, summer and winter, seedtime and harvest. They shall not cease." And Rayeh blessed Noah and his sons and said, "The awe and dread of you shall be upon every bird, beast, and creeping thing on the earth, even the fish of the sea. For as I gave you every green plant to eat, I now give you everything, only you shall not eat it with its blood. For its life is in the blood. I will require the life of a man who takes the life of another man. Again I say, 'be fruitful, multiply, and increase greatly upon the face of the earth." He paused, then continued, "Behold, I establish my covenant with you, your offspring after you, and every living creature with you. Never again shall all flesh be cut off by the waters of a flood. Never again will the earth be destroyed by a flood. Behold, this is the sign I give to you and all future generations. I have set my bow in the clouds and it shall be the sign of the covenant I have established for all time, between me and you and all the creatures of the earth." There in the sky, displayed for all to see, was the first rainbow. It was a beauty to behold.

And all dispersed to fulfill the command of Rayeh and live in the blessing of his covenant promises. Rayeh stood there alone until he was joined from behind by another. R'gal put his arm around his shoulder as he stepped up to his right side. He then drew Shenah from his scabbard as he knelt beside Reyah to plunge it tip first into the grass beneath his knee. With both hands on the hilt he proclaimed, "To the new beginning of all things good." He stood, pulled the sword from the earth, wiped the dirt off its blade on his tunic and replaced it in its scabbard. A portal opened to their right. He placed his left arm around Rayeh's shoulders, as Rayeh place his right around R'gal's, and together they walked through the portal.

This ends the First Book
of
The Adventures of R'gal
the Archangel

Glossary of Names

Adah - Lamech's wife, mother of Noah

Addar - One of R'gal's commanders

Alak - one of Lucifer's five kings

Alathos - the centaur, forger of the singing swords, etc.

Amthael - the proclaimed king of men

Balar - angel promoted to archangel by Lucifer

Boker - Uriel's sword of the first light, Dawn

Chayeem - the Tree of Life (Laughter)

Cozbi - daughter of Amthael's first counselor and Raziel's consort

Dakak - one of Lucifer's five kings

Elah - Haniel and Judith's half angelic son

Enoch - Jared's son and Japhia's husband

Ereveem - Japhia's granddaughter

Eshair - Michael's sword of questioning

Gabriel - an archangel who talks a lot, sword is Kol

Gareb - one of Lucifer's five kings

Halel - Lucifer's other name

Helel - Lucifer's sword of brightness, the Bright Star

Hane - Haniel's sword of favor

Haniel - an archangel, the comedian with the sword Hane

Hashak - one of Raziel's angel guards

Hathath - the fallen angel who sires the Ariel

Japhia - Elah's bethrothed who becomes Enoch's wife

Jaroah - one of Haniel's and Judith's maids

Jepheh - Enoch's wine steward and Methuselah's wife

Jephi - an angel who accompanies Dawn as a gazelle out of the Garden

Jubal - Master of music, inventor of stringed instruments

Jubiel - one of Haniel's commanders

Judith - Princess and Haniel's wife

Juniel - Noah's servant, friend of Regem (R'gal)

Kadaroot - One of Raziel's angel guards

Kol - Gabriel's sword of tender thunder

Koor - one of Raziel's commanders

Labah - one of the other two Ariel

Labee - the first Ariel produced by Hathath

Laesh - one of the other two Ariel

Lamech - Methuselah's son, Noah's father

Lucifer - Prince of the archangels, a little full of himself with the sword Helel

Mashal - daughter of Taphilla, wife to Noah's son Ham

Mekaroth - Raziel's half angel son, head of the Ashereem

Meraiah - Spokesman of R'gal's commanders

Meshkel - daughter of Taphilla, wife to Noah's son Shem

Methuselah - Enoch's son named, "When he is gone IT will come"

Michael - an archangel, who looks like the Father with the sword, Eshair

Naamah - Noah's wife, mother to his three sons

Noah - Lamech's son by his wife Adah

Nood - one of Lucifer's five kings

Oz - Raziel's sword of revelation of Glory

Princess - R'gal as a female Saluki (dog) for Japhia

Raash - one of Lucifer's five kings

Raphael - an archangel, the health nut with the sword Taan

Ratah - R'gal as Elah's tutor

Rayeh - the boy in the Tree, teacher of the archangels, and…

Rayneh - Adah's granddaughter, wife to Japheth

Raziel - an archangel, the mysterious one with the sword Oz

Regem - R'gal as a man helping Noah

Reggie - R'gal as a Basenji (dog) for Judith & Elah

R'gal - an archangel, slain in the rebellion, originally has the sword Yaman, later given Shenah

Robsar - smithy in the wilderness forging swords of wonder

Rolf - R'gal as a Basenji (dog) for Lamech

Shadai - daughter to one of the princes of men

Shamair - daughter of king Amthael

Shenah - R'gal's new sword of change

Shamah - one of R'gal's commanders

Soosa - the first mare, female horse

Taan - Raphael's sword of precision, the only female one

Taphilla - daughter of Jubal and Ereveem, with a beautiful voice

Tidal - one of Haniel's commanders

Tilon - one of R'gal's commanders

Tubal-Cain - Lamech's son

Tudar - one of Raziel's commanders

Uriel - an archangel, light on his feet with the sword Bokor

Yaman - R'gal's first sword, the sword of my right hand

Zach - an angel who accompanies Adam as a stallion out of the Garden

Zadok - one of Haniel's commanders

Zedekeem - the stones of Rightness

Zillah - Lamech's wife, grandmother of Naamah, Noah's wife

About the Author

William Siems, "Bill" to his friends, seems to have started telling stories as soon as he could talk. His wife says he still tends to share the truth creatively and with a flair for the dramatic. He grew up in south Seattle and has lived in Tacoma, Washington since 1972.

He worked nine years in hospitals, completing half his RN education. If you had a heart attack, he says he could half save you. Bill joined the Boeing Airplane Company in 1979. The last 15 years of his 32-year career he taught Employee and Leadership Development. Bill often developed and taught his own material. This led to writing numerous short stories and dramas, culminating in his first published novel *Amidst the Stones of Fire* in 2017 and its sequel *Out of the Sanctuary* in 2018.

A Biblical Adventure series followed, named *The Chayeem Chronicles.* It begins with the Christmas adventure *The Magi and a Lady,* and the gospel adventures *Hane and the Centurion*, and *Zach and a Guy Named Joe*, a rewriting of the first part of the book of Acts.

This is the debut of his next series *The Adventures of R'gal the Archangel*, called *The Sword Shenah.*

Now retired, Bill spends his time teaching, mentoring, writing, acting in community theater, and enjoying his family. Bill and his wife Nancy, of more than fifty years, live near their three children and seven grandchildren.

If you can't find Bill in his home office, with pages from his next book strewn all over the floor, then he is probably across the street playing with the neighbor's dog, Stacy, to whom he is Dogfather.

Made in United States
Troutdale, OR
12/30/2023

16548304R00176